For Debra, who has completed me.

Contents

And Satan answered the LORD, and said, Skin for skin, yea, all that a man hath will he give for his life.

The Book of Job
Chapter Two: Verse Four

Prologue

She was seven years old when the Shouting People came. It was early morning, which meant that everyone else in the mid-terrace, two-up-two-down was asleep. She was awake because children do not sleep late. The world outside was quiet, and dark enough for her to switch on the lights as she made her way downstairs from her tiny bedroom to the even smaller kitchen. It wasn't night-time dark. This was a special dark that didn't last long but was her favourite kind. This dark was a friendly dark, comfortable and comforting. It was *her* dark.

The girl pushed aside the dirty crockery and empty cups that littered the short, battered worktop as she searched out a plate, knife, and glass. Balancing precariously on a chair, she washed them under the tap, difficult because the sink was piled high with yet more dirty plates and cups. Satisfied that her utensils were clean, the girl set to work on a jam sandwich. There were a few slices of bread left in the pack. They were dry and hard, but she didn't mind. The jam would make it taste perfect. Jam made everything perfect. She poured herself a glass of cola, skilfully manoeuvring the mouth of the big plastic bottle over the rim of the tumbler then jerking it back and upwards before it overfilled.

Feast prepared, she went into the living room and, after checking that there were no sharp things hidden in its pile, sat, cross-legged, on the grubby carpet. Whenever she was awake, Mum would warn her about sharp things. "That bastard leaves his fucking needles everywhere," she would growl. "You be careful, sweetheart." Then Mum would ruffle her hair. The girl liked that. It meant that Mum was happy. She also liked the comforting tang of Mum's cigarette smoke, her chesty laugh and tangle of dirty blonde of hair. Mum was thin. When Mum hugged her, the girl could feel her bones. Her skin was always a little damp and she shook. Sometimes it was only a small tremor, other times it was so hard Mum had to hug herself and clench her teeth together to stop them chattering while she rocked backwards and forwards and talked to herself.

That morning, the morning of the Shouting People, Mum was asleep, and the girl knew enough to understand that she would be asleep for most of the day. Mum was on the sofa, tangled up with Bon, a tall, scruffy looking man with a shaved head and earrings and tattoos on his arms and all over his neck and face. The girl didn't like Bon. He frightened her because he acted as if she didn't exist and would sometimes just barge past her and knock her over and not say sorry or even look at her. And when he *did* look at her, the girl could see that he hated her.

Bon wasn't the only man who tangled himself with Mum on the sofa or the bed or the floor (the girl couldn't remember Mum or whoever she was with, checking the carpet for sharp things. Perhaps they didn't feel them or were safe from them because they were grown up). Some of the men were kind to her. One of them, Kurt, laughed a lot, always bought her sweets and sticker-books, and would sometime sit and watch a video with her. Kurt liked *The Jungle Book* and would sing along, although he had a terrible voice. The girl never told him, though, because he was kind and she didn't want to hurt his feelings. He was a big man with long hair and lots of muscles and only had tattoos on his arms. He never touched her or hugged her, but she knew that he liked her a lot. Kurt stopped coming after last Christmas. There had been a phone call and Mum had cried so loudly it was almost a scream. Her nose had run, and her eyes went as red as blood and she used one of the needles off the floor to put herself to sleep for days.

When the girl asked her what was wrong, Mum mumbled something about Kurt going to Heaven. It didn't make sense, so the girl thought she meant prison. Two of the men who had come around here were in prison, or perhaps the word was Devon, wherever that was. They teacher at school had talked about Devon. Devon was nice, according to Mrs Kahn. The girl didn't get to school much. She liked it a great deal, but if her school clothes were all dirty and Mum was asleep, she couldn't get there. Even if she wore dirty clothes, she still couldn't go because she wasn't supposed to walk there on her own.

School was bright and clean. All the women teachers wore makeup all the time and different clothes every day. Their voices were soft, sometimes loud, of course, but mostly soft. They didn't have a rough edge to their voices like Mum. And she never saw them smoking or injecting medicine into themselves.

One of the other men who came around to the flat was kind too, but not in a way the girl liked. Not in the way Kurt was kind. The other kind man did want to cuddle her and for her to sit on his lap while he smoked his cigarette. He managed to cuddle her once and the girl didn't like where his hands went. It frightened her and she managed to wriggle free and run up to her bedroom before he could cuddle her again. His cigarettes smelled different to Mum's cigarettes and made the girl dizzy. He would take a long suck at them then pass them to Mum. The girl didn't like the way Mum giggled when she smoked those funny cigarettes.

Of all the videos she owned, the girl liked *The Little Mermaid* best. She thought that Ariel, the mermaid in the film, was brave and beautiful. Mum loved that film too and always cried when Ariel burst upwards out of the sea, her tail magicked into legs and ready to find her true love on dry land.

On that morning, before it was really morning and the world was quiet and not-dark-but-not-light, the girl took The Little Mermaid from its battered case with its faded and blurred black-and-white picture on the front and pushed it into the slot of the video machine.

Just as Ariel burst out of the waves in the way that made Mum cry, someone banged on the front door and shouted at the top of their voice.

The door opened from the street, straight into the living room, which made the noise even louder. The shouter sounded angry, as if he wanted to beat-up everyone in the house. The banging turned into a hammering sound.

"Police," the man shouted. "Open up. Police."

Then the hammering stopped, and a slower, louder thumping noise began.

One.

The girl couldn't move. She stared at the front door. She felt something wet and realised that she had peed herself.

Two.

The girl began to shake. She wanted to cry and scream but she couldn't. It was as if she had been frozen in ice.

Three.

Crash.

The shouting invaders burst into the living room the way Ariel had burst out of the sea. They wore black-and-yellow and had helmets and were yelling, ordering people around and breaking things.

The girl saw one of them drag Bon off Mum and onto the floor. He groaned and cried. Then two others grabbed mum and hauled her to her feet then shoved her onto her knees. The girl looked into her mum's eyes. They were red and wide. Her mouth was open and there was a thin line of drool hanging from her lips like the strand of a shiny spider web.

The shouting invaders, who the girl now realised were policemen and women, tied Bon and mum up with their hands behind their backs. They crashed and bashed around the house, downstairs and up. They opened things and pulled things over and tore them up. One of them laughed and said to Mum and Bon that even if they didn't find any drugs, they could be nicked for possession of enough pirate videos to open a new branch of Blockbusters.

The girl was confused. They didn't have any pirate videos. They had Disney films and sloppy films that made Mum cry and funny ones that made Mum laugh. But no pirate ones. She wanted to tell the policeman that he was wrong, but she couldn't speak. It felt as if her tongue had swollen up so big it filled her whole mouth and stopped any words coming out.

Then someone yelled from the bedroom that they had *found it*.

Everything went quiet. Mum was breathing very fast, her breath all raspy. She was hunched forward as if she had a tummy ache. Bon had stopped swearing and shrieking and was also breathing hard. The girl was glad he was stuck on his tummy and she hoped that the thin black plastic strip that bound his hands was so tight it really hurt.

Everything stopped.

The girl heard car doors open and shut outside. An aeroplane scratched and whined through the sky.

The front door opened, and two more people came in. A woman in a smart coat and black suit and a large man in a grey suit who didn't have much hair. The others called the woman Ma'am.

There was a lot of talking. One of the policemen showed Ma'am a handful of needles and some bags of the white powder that Mum said was her medicine. Ma'am looked angry then sad. She gave an order. The girl tried to understand but their voices were just noise now. She couldn't make out any words. She was still sitting in front of the television, still watching *The Little Mermaid*, the scary part where the wicked sea-witch had cast a spell on Ariel's father.

Then the girl felt a hand on her shoulder and jumped. She looked up to see one of the policewomen crouched beside her.

"What's your name?" she said. The policewoman's voice was so soft and kind that it almost made the girl cry. But she was going to be brave like Ariel. So, she forced herself to speak in a clear, certain voice and said, "Eve Clement."

Chapter One: St Jude

When the two-carriage train growled its way out of the tiny station, it left, in its wake, a silence so profound that it was more white-roar than quietness.

An icy wind sliced along the empty platform and snapped at the Reverend Eve Clement's coat. It scoured her face and tugged at her thick mane of unruly red hair until she was forced to pull up the hood of her parka. Suddenly the world was framed in an oval of fake fur. It was better that way, she decided.

Empty was the word for this place. She hadn't realised that such out-of-the-way railway stations still existed. There had been no sign of Weddon village when the train had slowed for its approach, just an impenetrable wall of trees. Eve didn't like it here. The isolation and quiet were claustrophobic. She wanted some noise, bustle, activity. As for the silence, she was afraid of silence. She didn't know it or want it. Silence was too empty and, therefore, too easily filled.

"Hi, are you Reverend Clements?" Though muffled by the parka's hood, the voice was loud enough to snatch Eve's attention.

She turned to see a tall, dark-haired woman walking towards her. The woman was wrapped in a heavy and expensive-looking coat.

"Yes, I am."

"Sorry I'm late," the woman said. She held out a hand, which was encased in a soft leather glove. "I'm Angela Pullman. Deacon at St Jude's."

Deacon? This elegant, glamorous woman was a deacon?

And why shouldn't she be?

Eve realised that she was the consummate Londoner, unable to believe that elegance and fashion existed beyond the M25, especially out here in what her few remaining friends at St Martin's had blasphemously called the Far Side of East Jesus.

"Pleased to meet you," Eve answered and pushed back the parka's hood.

"And you." Angela's smile was warm. She nodded towards Eve's single suitcase. "Is that all your luggage?"

"Yes. That's my life, apart from my books and my laptop. I sent those ahead. You did say that the rectory is furnished."

"Absolutely. You'll be glad to know your books arrived safely. I took the liberty of setting things up for you. I hope you don't mind. I thought that bed-making and playing hunt-the-kettle would the last thing you'd want after your journey here."

"Thanks, I really appreciate that."

Angela took Eve's arm and they headed for the station exit. A simple act of comfort but one that almost broke the fragile wall of Eve's self-control. There had been too little comfort of late.

"You surprised that I'm your deacon?" Angela said as she guided Eve across the small car park.

"I was. I suppose…"

"I know you Londoners believe that in the backwoods men are men and women know their place."

"Maybe. A little."

Angela laughed. "There's still some of that around, but the modern world has even managed to catch up with us here"

"There's *some of that* in London too, believe you me," Eve said.

Angela's car was a soft-top MX5. This time Eve was not surprised. Angela drove fast and confidently. They met no other vehicles as they left the station. Eve was puzzled by this. She had holidayed in the sticks many times when she was a child but had never experienced such emptiness. It wasn't just the traffic. There were no houses either, no farms, no buildings of any kind. The hedges flashed by and through the gaps she glimpsed an endless vista of rolling brown fields.

Angela chatted; small talk that put Eve at her ease. She was single, she said, and intended to remain that way. "Not for me, marriage." There was that laugh again. Infectious, a little abandoned, perhaps. "What about you? What's your take on the estate of holy matrimony?"

"I believe in it. I also believe that it is ordained by God. Our natural state."

Hypocrite. That silent voice again. Conscience? If so, she was cursed with a surprisingly sarcastic one.

A moment, as Angela appeared to ponder Eve's reply. Then; "Ah, an old-fashioned answer. And a careful one."

Rumbled. From sarcastic to smug. Her conscience was not

someone she wanted to spend an evening with.

"It's okay. I'm teasing. Look, Eve, I know about you. I've done my research. You wouldn't have been called here if we had a problem with you."

"Thank you. I appreciate that. In fact, I don't think you have any idea of just how much I appreciate it."

Angela's hand came to rest, briefly, on Eve's knee. Far from being an imposition, the contact was welcome and, once again, comforting. "You'll be happy here. I promise."

She believed it, until she saw the church and the vicarage.

She experienced a moment of panic. She couldn't do this. She wanted to go back to London. Now. This minute.

St Jude's was a lonely, ancient building with a simple, circular Norman tower. It was set back, about a hundred yards from the road and, apart from the adjacent, equally ancient rectory, there were no other houses in sight. Not even a barn or electricity pylon and very few trees, except for an isolated copse on the far side of the field that fronted the cottage. The land sloped gently away in all other directions. Nothing but expanses of ploughed earth, divided up by lines of scrappy hedgerow. It was brown, desolate and unutterably lonely.

Eve climbed from the car and was immediately punched by a fierce gust of cold wind that swept in from the east. Heavy grey cloud boiled overhead. A few drops of icy rain stung her face. Then she felt Angela's hand on her shoulder, and it was, again, comfort from a simple gesture.

"It isn't as bad as it looks," Angela said as she led the way to the rectory door. "I was here when the removal van arrived. Everything's in its place. I lit a fire earlier and there's a casserole in the slow-cooker."

"But I don't own a slow-cooker."

"You do now. Think of it as a welcoming gift. The casserole should be done by now."

"Thank you, I don't know what to say. It's very kind of you." Eve felt brighter when she noticed the smoke curling from the cottage's chimney. She could smell it too, woody, oddly familiar and welcoming.

"I'd like to see the church before I go in," Eve said. "It's the reason I'm here, after all."

Angela looked a little surprised, but then she smiled. "Of course. I understand. I've got the key with me here."

The door opened without so much as a creak. It took a quick search for Eve to locate the bank of light switches to the left of the doorway. The church seemed even smaller on the inside than it looked from the outside. The walls were plain white. The roof was low, and supported by dark-stained, wooden beams. The seating consisted of rows of ancient, uncomfortable-looking pews. Many churches had replaced such seating with modern chairs. She would investigate that. No point in a congregation being physically uncomfortable.

A hymn board hung from the wall, displaying the numbers of the last hymns sung before her arrival. The hymnals themselves, piled neatly at the end of each pew, looked old and battered. No modern gospel music here. St Jude's was a place of traditional hymns, accompanied, presumably, by the modest-sized pipe organ situated on the left of the nave.

She warmed to the place. There was a reverence in the old language of the hymnals. There was also a simplicity and honesty about the minimalist lines of the church itself. St Jude's was not built to intimidate. There was little show or pomp.

The pulpit was old, but functional. She glimpsed an enormous bible, open on its lectern. Without looking, she knew it would be a King James and not a modern translation.

She moved towards the altar, which was dressed in a spotless white cloth and bore a gleaming gold cross flanked by two equally impressive communion chalices.

And there was the window.

Where tradition stopped.

If this was a biblical scene recreated in the coloured glass, then it was one Eve had missed during her dozen or so read-throughs over the years. A story from the Apocrypha perhaps? She had read that too and, again, nothing sprang to mind.

Central to the image was a woman, in profile, leaning over a well. The woman wore the kind of hooded robes that were standard in Biblical representations and were coloured green, edged with gold. The woman's head was covered, which rendered her face invisible. The well was little more than a hole in the ground, edged with rough grey paving. The background was of rolling desert, featureless and bland, apart from a bank of clouds gathered over the horizon. A storm was coming. Eve could feel it, a remarkable effect for a stained-glass image.

A bare and muscular arm extended from the mouth of the well. The woman grasped it with both her hands and appeared to be in the act of trying to pull its unfortunate owner out of the hole.

There was something unwholesome about the darkness of that pit. A solidity. A completeness that made her shudder. There was also something disturbing about the arm that reached out from it. Nothing Eve could define. Just…a feeling.

Tiredness, that was what.

"It's beautiful and strange at the same time," she said.

"Yes, it is,"

"What does it mean?"

Angela shrugged. "The gospel. The church pulling the sinner out of the darkness."

The answer made sense. After all, the church was often described as the Bride of Christ, which gave it a female aspect. Reasonable as it was, Angela's explanation didn't make Eve feel any better about the image. She needed to see the woman's face. The need was an irritant that put her on edge. Why had the artist hidden her? What games was he (or she) playing? What sort of idiotic, bloody joke was being perpetrated here?

Appalled at her anger, Eve turned away to break the link that had formed between herself and the window.

"I'm cold," she lied. "Let's get in the warm."

*

The casserole's meaty aroma pervaded the entire ground floor. A fire crackled in the large sitting room fireplace, around which worn-but-inviting armchairs and a tatty old two-seat sofa had been placed. Within moments of Eve sitting down to warm herself, Angela was back with two mugs of coffee. She hadn't asked Eve's preferences, but she had guessed correctly: white, one sugar.

Which disturbed her a little. Angela was almost too good to be true. Ridiculous. Eve knew that she should be glad of the support, not questioning it.

"I'll need fire-lighting instructions," she said as she pushed off her boots and curled her toes before the flames. She still wore her coat, too tired to remove it. "I've never lived in a house with an open fire and we're not allowed them in London anyway."

"It's easy enough. I'll show you later."

"How far are we from Weddon village?" Eve asked.

"A couple of miles," Angela said. She had taken the opposing armchair. "It's separated from the church because of the Black Death. The original village was burned down to stop the spread of the plague and rebuilt a few miles away. It happened a lot."

Angela's eyes locked with Eve's. Her gaze was intense, unnerving, and filled with something Eve couldn't name. Or didn't want to.

Angela drained her coffee and stood. "Let's eat. I don't know about you, but I'm starving."

*

Eve was alone.

Angela had gone home and suddenly there was no one in the house with her or going about their business outside. No background city-roar here. No traffic noise. She was the only person in this place. The emptiness, the solitude, the sheer white, impenetrable wall of nothingness bore down on her. If anything happened, there would be no shouting for help, no rushing out into the street for assistance.

She picked up her mobile phone.

No signal.

Eve stared at the device and for a moment it was beyond comprehension that there could be a place where a mobile phone was useless.

Then, suddenly, she was angry with herself for being so helplessly pathetic. There was nothing out there that could do her any harm. She was safer here than she could ever be in a teeming metropolis like London.

But loneliness was loneliness.

The fire burned low but still gave off heat. The room was lit by a single standard lamp which gave it a comfortable, intimate feel. The wind outside had become a gale. Rain hammered at the windows.

So, why had she been invited to take up the stewardship of this church in particular? It was an unlikely placement for someone like her, a city-soaked Londoner with the River Thames flowing through her veins. To say that this parish was the polar opposite of Eve's previous church, St Martin's, looked like being the understatement of the century.

But then, this wasn't so much a placement as exile. She was out of the way here, Out of trouble.

She needed to walk to the village tomorrow and get a feel for the place. Of course, there would be suffering in this parish; loneliness, depression, and isolation, particularly for any elderly people living outside the village boundaries. And what of the youth? Were there jobs in the area? What was there for them to do at night and at the weekends? Their frustration and sense of powerlessness must be monumental. Eve allowed herself a small smile. There would be plenty of work for her here.

A log snapped in the fireplace. Eve started awake. She had dozed. She should get to bed. First though, she would pray. Always a struggle, prayer. It was a spiritual battle. A fight to hold onto enough faith to speak to the darkness behind her eyes and believe that someone was listening. Since the death of Ruth, the struggle had intensified into an act of pure faith, because she no longer experienced any sense of a divine presence. But she had to believe. She had to hang onto the shreds of her faith, because without them she was nothing.

She slid from the chair to kneel on the rug before the fireplace. The moment her legs touched the soft pile – no needles in this mat – she was wrenched back to the moment she prayed for the first time in her life. It snatched away her breath.

There were too many raw spots in Eve's memory. Some of them lay so close to the surface that they would suddenly burst through – like Ariel bursting out of the waves – and consume her. Anything could trigger such a flashback, a smell, a sound, a voice or snatch of music. Films and television programmes were strong stimulants.

There was one film she could never watch again.

The Little Mermaid.

The film, shown at a schoolfriend's eleventh birthday party, four years after the Invasion of the Shouting People, had given Eve nightmares for a week. It broke her down into helpless sobbing when she tried to confront it as an adult. Eve didn't often cry. When she did, it was like the collapse of her entire physical, mental and spiritual self.

The memories, roughly buried in the shallow grave of her consciousness, were a sensory slideshow, a formless jumble of impressions, sounds and smells. And now, kneeling on the floor of her new home, she remembered that first prayer and how frightening it had been.

Because someone was there.

In the darkness behind her tightly closed eyes, she had whispered Dear Lord Jesus, just as New Mum instructed, and a voice answered her.

I am here, Eve.

It wasn't a loud voice. It wasn't a voice she could hear with her ears. It wasn't a man or woman's voice. It was…in her head. She was startled and afraid, but not so afraid that she opened her eyes or cried out. The voice wasn't going to hurt her. It belonged to something vast, something that filled *everything* and *everywhere*.

She didn't wonder how it knew her name.

"Hello," she said in a small, quavery voice.

"Sorry?" New Mum sounded amused. "Did you just say hello to Jesus?"

Eve opened her eyes, turned to New Mum who was on her knees beside her, and saw that she was smiling. She seemed to smile a lot. Eve nodded, uncertain of what New Mum would do or say.

She chuckled. "Well, I suppose it's as good a way as any to get to know Him."

"He was there," Eve said.

New Mum's smile faltered. She stared hard at Eve. Then laid a gentle hand on Eve's shoulder. She seemed to find it difficult to speak. "Yes," she said after a moment. "He is." She sniffed then smiled again. "Let's finish our prayer, shall we?"

Another nod from Eve, because she wasn't sure what she was supposed to say.

"Let me teach you a prayer," New Mum said. "Are you ready? All right. It goes like this. Jesus, tender shepherd, hear me, bless thy little lamb tonight. In the darkness be thou near me and keep me safe till morning light."

Eve closed her eyes but, this time, only heard New Mum's voice. She was disappointed but decided she would try again tomorrow night.

"Is there anyone you want to pray for?" New Mum said.

"Mum."

"Of course."

"And Kurt."

"All right. What do you want to ask Jesus to do for them?"

"Please, Jesus, will you look after Mum and make her come back and look after Kurt in Devon."

"That's nice," New Mum said. She looked as if she wanted to say something. Instead, she smiled her warm, soft smile and got to her feet. She was a tall, pretty woman with long blonde hair. Her name was Sandra, but she asked Eve to call her mummy. Eve answered, as politely as she could (Mum had always told her to be polite) that she didn't like saying mummy and that she, Sandra, wasn't her mum. Could she call her New Mum? Sandra smiled her smile and said that New Mum was perfectly fine.

This was Eve's third night at her new home.

She had a new Dad as well, although she couldn't remember having an old one. This one was named Paul and he was the same height as Sandra. He looked like John Craven who presented *Newsround* on television. He smiled a lot too and laughed and Eve could tell that he liked games and jokes. New Dad agreed with New Mum that she should say her prayers each night. They also went to church every Sunday morning and were going to take Eve with them. She was intrigued because she had no idea what a church was. There would be singing, apparently. She liked singing.

Eve was happy here, so far. She liked New Mum and New Dad. She felt safe. But it was different to her home. She missed Mum. She missed her smoky smell and rough voice and the way she ruffled her hair and called her *love* and *doll* and *sweet-cheeks*. She missed making jam sandwiches early in the morning and eating them while she watched videos. She didn't think she could do that here, even though New Mum and New Dad had all her favourites and more in the big cabinet under the giant television in the sitting room.

When she went to bed she wanted to cry, because it was then that she missed Mum most. But she didn't. She had to be brave and that night she felt brave because she believed that she had found a friend. Out there in the dark. When she prayed.

New Mum and New Dad had been the last confusion at the end of the frightening chaotic jumble of faces, places and voices that followed the morning of the Shouting People. Even now, almost thirty years later, she could feel, see, and hear all of it. It was easily summoned and hard to put away. Imprinted most vividly was Mum's face. The realisation that had seeped its way into that the miasma of heroin fuzz, that she was about to lose her daughter. It started as the word *no*. A quiet, almost whispered *no* in that husky, ruined voice of hers. Then it became a shout then a scream. Something like the agonised howls of an animal when it feels the jaws of a predator close about its throat.

It took three police officers to get her out of the room. She kicked and struggled and bit and spat and squealed and shrieked. Eve sat on the floor with the kind policewoman's hand on her shoulder holding her in place. Eve tried to understand. She knew that she should shout too. That she should kick and bite, but she couldn't move.

She could only watch.

Then listen as the sounds faded and dissolved into the roar of morning rush-hour traffic outside.

"Mum," Eve had said then, a quiet, almost whispered word that tore a bloodied chunk of meat from her heart.

"Mum," she said tonight, in front of the fire in the cottage-rectory in Weddon, and felt another chunk torn loose and hurled into the darkness.

The embers of the fire were hot on her face. Their smoky perfume was the incense of purification. She breathed it in and let it unfurl in her mind, tendrils of mist that reached in and prised her soul from her flesh.

Resigned to yet another session of agonised, unheeded pleading she whispered; "I need you, God."

Eve, I am here –

Eve snapped opened her eyes and scrambled to her feet. The intensity of His presence was sudden and terrifying. She stumbled back from the fire and bumped up against the armchair hard enough to drop back into its embrace. Breathing hard, she tried to make sense of what she had experienced. It was as if someone had turned an amplifier up to full volume while she stared into the beam of a searchlight.

There could be no more prayer tonight. She knew that she should be full of joy. Instead, she was afraid.

*

The bed looked soft and inviting. Eve muttered a heartfelt thanks to Angela then crossed to the bedroom window. She made to draw the curtains.

And hesitated.

The window looked out over fields. By peering round to her right, Eve could see part of St Jude's tower, flood-lit like all parish churches, since the Queen's Silver Jubilee back in 1977. The spotlight's orange glow gave the illusion that the light came from within the stony walls themselves. More light spilled from the lamp onto the hedge that separated the driveway from the fields beyond. The tangled, winter-bare branches broke it into a jagged patchwork of light and shadow.

Someone was out there in the liquid blackness that shrouded the field.

Eve couldn't see who it was, but she knew. She could feel their presence.

Unnerved, she grabbed the old, heavy curtains and made to draw them shut. The glass rattled as rain was hurled against it. The wind howled then quietened, a relentless wax and wane.

A figure stepped forward, blurred by the rain; dark, indistinct, as if formed from the shadows in which it had hidden. A woman who appeared to be wearing a track suit. Her hair blew wildly. She raised her arm in greeting.

Mum.

No, it couldn't be. Dear God, no.

Fighting for breath, Eve slid to the floor. She sat against the wall under the window, arms tight about herself. The need to take another look was overwhelming but had to be resisted. To look again was an admission that she was seeing things that were not there in the jigsaw chaos of light and dark. On the other hand, to crouch here like a frightened child and not face down her own imagination was no good either.

It was not Mum.

Mum was dead.

It. Was. Not. Mum.

Slowly, she uncoiled herself, took a breath then peered outside.

The figure was still there.

Close to the house now, clearly visible in the wash of light from the church.

Eve ran.

She clattered down the stairs too fast. They were narrow, steep and dangerous. She didn't care. She made it to the bottom without accident and crashed into the hall. She fought the lock and wrenched open the front door then stumbled out wearing no coat and heedless of the rain.

"Mum."

There was no figure. No Mum, only shifting shadow that splintered then reformed in the orange light of the floodlights.

Eve felt the lash of the storm for the first time. The wind shoved at her like a playground bully and it was cold. She didn't care. Another step. She caught a scent, wet material, wet hair. Then the briefest, faintest waft of cheap perfume.

The smells faded and the emptiness they left behind was unbearable. Eve slumped against the door frame and sobbed Mum's name over and over again. She hadn't come back. She would never come back. It was the storm, exhaustion, loneliness.

Then there was light, brighter than the Queen's Jubilee floodlights. It blazed from the church windows and tore the night to shreds. There was someone in there.

Eve ran to building, arm up to protect her face from the glare and from the rain. She was afraid. It could be vandals or thieves. It could be…She had to know. The door was open. She stumbled inside.

It took a moment for Eve to realise that the light did not come from the electric lamps, but from the big stained-glass window at the end of the nave, above the altar. She tried to look into the glare, eyes partially closed. It was like trying to stare directly at the sun.

There was a sound too. Voices, joined in deafening harmony, beautiful, sublime. Eve grabbed at the nearest of the pews for support, crying once again, the outpouring of grief triggered by her memories and imagined glimpses of Mum.

Painful as it was, her gaze was drawn to the inferno of colour exploding from the window. The voices rose in volume and intensity.

A figure emerged from the light. Human, yet inhuman. Winged. Vast. Awful. Glorious –

Chapter Two: St Martins

Was He there *that* Sunday? God?

Was He there on that Sunday when *she* came?

Odd how the links of a chain are formed, Eve told herself many months later. Unrelated events, invisible threads drawing the edges of the cloth together.

It was an ordinary, nondescript, sabbath. One Eve would have forgotten if the blonde woman hadn't walked into St Martin's and taken her seat near the front.

Eve was tired that evening. The weariness was a physical weight that bore down on her shoulders. She was unwell. It felt like flu. She suffered a near-permanent headache. She needed a break, but the work had to go on. These people needed her. The people looking expectantly up at her at her as she stood in the pulpit. There was so much work still to do. She couldn't stop now.

Those above gave her little support. It was as if the success of her ministry at St Martin's was an embarrassment. She had always been a troublesome priest; outspoken on social issues, treading too close to politics, getting her hands dirty. St Martin's was, she knew, a form of exile. A run-down parish in an impoverished borough of North London where she could be mislaid and, hopefully, lost.

She was alone in this and not sure that she had much more to give.

The blonde woman was remarkable because, for the most part, Eve's flock was not as well-dressed as she was. They didn't have the money, or the energy, for such niceties. Charity Shops and supermarket cut-price were their boutiques. For too many of them, food banks were their corner shops. And, up until recently, religion had been an irrelevance, a meaningless and incomprehensible something that neither affected their lives nor interested them in the slightest.

But here they were here in church, singing hymns, praying and listening to sermons, because, they said, Eve had reached out to them. She had made it her business to get to know everyone in the downtrodden desolation of this parish, the same desolation she, herself, had been born into, and they had responded. At last, someone cared. Someone rode the piss-stinking lifts to the upper floors of the tower blocks where many of them lived. Someone ventured out into the freezing winter dark to deliver soup and sandwiches and hot drinks to the shop doorways and other dark holes in which many slept. Someone was prepared to talk to the drug-addled, the drink-ruined, the poor, lonely and downtrodden and offer friendship and something else that was hard for them to define. When the Lady Rev, as she had been named, came to call, she brought a little hope with her.

But each act of kindness each new initiative, each good work, drained a tiny measure of energy from her spirit. Giving to those who could never give back was a one-way draw on her strength and it felt as though it was failing. For a moment, standing in the battered old pulpit of that battered and neglected old church in its battered and neglected parish, Eve could not find the words she needed to open the service. The warm, still air suddenly seemed thin. She couldn't breathe. There was too much to do. There were too many people in need. She didn't know where to start anymore. She couldn't do this.

Then the blonde woman smiled up at her and suddenly Eve was energised. It was ridiculous. One smile, one barely perceptible nod of encouragement and the barrier dissolved. Eve was able to call her congregation to prayer and once more lead them to God.

"That was a remarkable sermon, Reverend." Those were the first words the woman spoke to Eve. It was outside the church, after the service and during the traditional handshaking and greetings exchanged as the congregation filed out. People were never in a hurry to leave, especially on a pleasant evening like this and they milled around to talk and laugh in the narrow strip of graveyard that separated St Martin's from the street. The lingering evening light had turned deep gold. The sun was no longer visible behind the rooftops of the run-down shops and shabby terrace houses on the opposite side of the road.

"Thank you," Eve replied. "I don't believe we've met before."

"No, we haven't. Although I have visited one or two of the community projects you've set up –"

"*Helped* set up," Eve said. "I can't take all the credit."

The woman's regard was disarmingly direct. "I'm Ruth Chandler, prospective MP for this constituency."

Of course, there was an election in a month or so, which

meant that this was politics. Still, politician or not, there was something personable about Ruth Chandler.

"Dare I ask which side you're on?" Eve asked.

She was rewarded by a chuckle and warm smile. "Labour. Is that okay with you?"

"I'm apolitical," Eve answered, which wasn't quite true. She had, so far, always voted for Ruth's party.

"I admire you greatly," Ruth said.

Flattered as she was, Eve was put on the defensive by the comment. It seemed too fulsome. It carried the potential for insincerity, although, Ruth's smile looked to be genuine enough.

"I think we can be allies," Ruth continued. "I intend to shake things up even more than you have already. This is a rotten borough. Unfortunately, the constituency spreads into a more affluent area that makes it a safe seat for its sitting MP. They're the people he lives to please because they're the ones who vote."

"Not many people round here see any point in voting. They don't believe it will make any difference to their lives, no matter who gets in. I have to say that I'm inclined to sympathise with the view."

Ruth chuckled, a short, sweet burst of laughter. "But it won't be like that much longer, if I have my way."

Eve realised that Ruth was still holding her hand. Her grip was firm. Ruth moved a little closer. She held Eve's gaze. "I want us to work together. No politics, that wouldn't be right, but this place needs some help and you can't do this alone. You look tired, Reverend. I want you to know that you have an ally now."

Chapter Three: Woman At The Well

Eve woke, suddenly, breathing hard. It was daylight. She was confused and frightened. She didn't know where she was. The room was all wrong; sloped ceiling, exposed, dark-stained beams, unfamiliar wallpaper.

Cottage.

Rectory.

St Jude's.

She slumped back, unable to remember coming to bed. She had been…outside. The church. The light. A dream then. Vivid. One that had left an emotional mark. She felt residual grief and let the images flicker through her mind.

A sound.

There was someone downstairs. She thought she was alone out here, yet no one, living or dead, seemed inclined to leave her be. She struggled out of bed and was startled to see that she was still dressed, sans shoes and socks. Not good. There had been a short spell of going to bed fully dressed a year or so ago; a habit born of grief and the liquid salve she had turned to for comfort.

More angry than nervous, Eve stripped off her damp

clothes (damp?), grabbed the dressing gown, sweats and tee-shirt Angela had neatly folded into the bedroom's chest of drawers then went out onto the landing.

"Hello?"

"I've put the kettle on." Angela, in the kitchen by the sound of it. Eve was both relieved and annoyed. Relieved that there was someone here, but also irritated by the fact that Angela appeared to believe that she could simply let herself in when she felt like it.

Ah well. She might as well make the most of the company.

"I hope you don't mind," Angela said when Eve stepped into the kitchen. She was perfectly turned out in a thick roll neck jumper and expensive looking jeans. She stood at the ancient electric cooker, shuffling eggs and bacon around a frying pan. The smell of it was gorgeous. "I was worried about you."

"Worried?"

"Just a feeling." Angela turned to offer Eve a broad smile. There was light in that smile.

Light.

A memory snapped into Eve's mind. Light. The giant winged figure in the blazing window.

"Hey, why don't you sit down?" Angela was suddenly concerned. "You look pale."

"Why are you here? What..." Eve couldn't think. She was relieved to see Angela, yet, oddly, afraid of her.

"You need help. I came." Angela removed the frying pan from the heat then turned around to talk to Eve. She stood, arms folded, leaning against the kitchen work top. "Look, I didn't need to be a mind-reader to see that you were disorientated and a bit, well, shocked when you arrived here yesterday. I felt that I ought to make sure you were okay this morning."

"Thank you. I'm sorry, I didn't mean to, you know…"

"Don't even think about it," Angela said. "It's my job to take care of you."

She finished work on the breakfast and sat down at the table with Eve.

"You don't need me to tell you that Satan will visit you here," Angela said.

"He's an old friend."

"He?" Angela said. "Sorry, but how do you know that Satan is a *he*? These beings transcend sex. There are no male or female angels or devils. Sorry, being pedantic" She reached across the table to squeeze Eve's hand. "The important thing is that any servant of God worth their salt will attract the Devil's attention. Look, I know you've been through this before, in London, but out here, in the middle of nowhere, it might seem more…intense."

There was a second layer to Angela's words, a current that flowed beneath the surface. She knew something, about last night.

"You're right about that."

A pause. They ate, and sipped coffee.

"It's not just the presence of a righteous person that brings Satan to this place," Angela said.

"What do you mean?"

"St Jude's is, well it's special. The church is built on a particularly holy site. People are reputed to have visions here, of the Virgin Mary and other saints and prophets."

"Do you believe that?"

Angela shrugged. "Anything is possible where God is concerned."

And Eve remembered her own, what? Dream? Vision? Hallucination? The window, the winged figure. And the prayer, the unnerving presence of God.

"Are you sure you're alright Eve?"

"It's nothing. Really."

"Okay, I'd best be getting along."

"I might wander over to the village later," Eve said.

"Yes, of course. Bit of a walk though. I'd offer you a lift, but I need to run some errands."

Eve was puzzled by the remark. Hadn't Angela said, yesterday, that the village was only a couple of miles away? Well a couple of miles could mean anything, and she may have been trying to lessen Eve's initial shock at the remoteness of the place.

"No, it's fine," Eve said. "I need a walk. And I need a car. I'm not going to be able to visit my parishioners if I don't have one."

"You won't find a car dealer in Weddon, I'm afraid, but I'll put some feelers out. I'm sure we'll come up with something."

There it was again, a hint of obstructiveness. Almost as if Angela didn't want her to go into the village.

"Ah, all right. Thanks."

Angela pulled on the coat she had left on the back of the sofa and made for the door. She paused on the threshold, haloed by the bright winter sunlight. She looked back at Eve, who was now standing in front of the fire, relishing its heat on her legs.

"This is a big change for you," Angela said.

"I need the change."

And she did.

A few moments later, Eve heard the roar of Angela's sports car and then it was silent again and she was once more alone. She set to work on the washing up. Today was Wednesday. Four days until Sunday. She had sermons to prepare.

Angela had selected the second bedroom to act as Eve's office. It was directly opposite to Eve's own bedroom and next to the bathroom. It was small, but surprisingly warm and comfortable. A desk had been placed under its window, which gave yet another view of gentle rolling fields, all of them fallow for the winter. They stretched towards the horizon like a brown ocean of ploughed earth. There was a large clump of trees on the far side of the nearest field. Too small to be a wood and too large to be called a copse. The road curved into view on the right, then disappeared behind a high hedge.

The sky had cleared to bright winter blue. There was no sign of any breeze. It looked cold.

Eve picked up her Bible and it fell open at Job Chapter One. She recoiled. Tears stung her eyes. Was this some sort of joke?

Why that page? Why that Book?

Then she remembered the intensity of God's presence when she had attempted to pray last night. A small burst of joy so bright that it was almost euphoria burst through her. This was no joke. This was a message. This was intentional. She swallowed hard, composed herself and began to read.

"And Satan answered the Lord, and said, 'Skin for skin, yea, all that a man hath will he give for his life. But put forth thine hand now and touch his (Job's) bone and his flesh, and he will curse thee to thy face.'

"And the Lord said unto Satan, 'Behold, he is in thine hand; but save his life.'

"So went Satan forth from the presence of the Lord, and smote Job with sore boils from the sole of his foot unto his crown."

It was, on the face of it, a terrible story. A man's faith being tested in the most awful manner, boils, bereavement. All suggested by Satan and sanctioned by God himself. How could he do that? How could He listen to his enemy and allow himself to be drawn into such a savage game? It was almost like Professor Higgins' wager that he could turn Eliza Doolittle into a lady, only this time it was a man's life and family that were at stake.

It wasn't that simple, of course.

Another puzzle; Satan given access to God. All right, it was a morality tale, a parable, but the incongruity of that meeting had troubled her like a nagging tooth, ever since the night Ruth had questioned her on the story.

That night.

She clamped down hard on the memory and began her research, thumbing through commentaries, trying to get the bottom of this most difficult of Biblical narratives.

Tired of fighting to keep her emotions in check, she stopped and took a deep breath. There would be no crying. Crying was finished and done. She leaned back on her chair, looked out of the window.

And saw Mum.

She froze. The figure was in the middle of the field. Arm

raised as if to gain attention. She wore her scruffy track suit. The details were not that distinct, but Eve could see it was her.

She didn't hesitate.

The figure was still there when Eve stepped out through the back door. Mum, if Mum it was, and it couldn't be, had not moved. She stood, as if waiting.

Eve pulled on her wellingtons, a fever of tugging and cursing the stiff, brand new boots. She zipped up her parka against the cold, stepped outside and looked for an entrance into the field. There was none in sight, so she clambered into the ditch that bordered it, scrambled awkwardly out, and set off across the ripped-open earth.

Walking on a ploughed field was harder than she had imagined it would be. The churned clay had been curled into frozen waves. Between them there were deep grooves that threatened sprained ankles.

But still the figure waited.

Mum. Obviously, Mum. She was wearing her slippers here in this field, yet, unsuitable as they were, they didn't appear to cause her a problem.

But it was Mum.

Mum.

Stop, think. Stop. This could not be Mum.

Eve couldn't stop. She stumbled over the broken earth, tripped, almost fell, recovered. Then she did fall. She dropped heavily to her hands and knees, panting from the effort. What the hell was she doing? Chasing a hallucination, a delusion. A deception.

She stared down at the heavy curls of clay, afraid now to look up, afraid that the apparition was gone.

Getting to her feet wasn't easy. The ground itself seemed unsteady. The entire world shifted dizzily. She waited until the nausea passed, then looked up. There would be an empty field and that vast East Anglian sky, flawlessly, mercilessly blue and clear.

There was Mum. Perhaps ten yards or so away now.

Eve took a step towards her. Mum nodded then turned about and walked away.

No.

"Mum, wait. Please."

Eve increased her pace, heedless now of the lethal, frozen storm of broken earth over which she lurched and staggered. Walking easily despite her ridiculous footwear, Mum was making for the clump of trees that bordered the far end of the field. When she reached them, she stepped into their shadow and disappeared

Eve made it to the edge of the copse and paused. She was out of breath.

A moment, then, heart pumping so hard she was afraid it would give out, she ventured into the quiet, shaded space between the trees. The ground was clear but for a carpet of death-browned bracken. There was no breath of wind, no movement but her own. She glanced up at the sky, now webbed by the denuded branches.

No birds.

Yes, it was winter, but surely there should be some species of birds out here. She realised that she had not seen or heard any since she had arrived. There had to be an explanation, of course. There always was.

She walked slowly towards what she judged to be the

centre of the copse. She had an urge to be quiet, to creep through the trees. Ridiculous. There was no need for silence here. She quickened her pace. The ground was uneven but made soft by the winter-dead undergrowth. The place was surprisingly light.

And there she was. Standing between the huge, gnarled trunks of a pair of oak trees. Her hands were in the pockets of her tatty tracksuit pants. She stared hard at Eve as she approached. Closer now. More detail; her dirty blonde hair, the sharp angles of her face. And there was that expression, hard yet edged with softness that always broke through when she saw her daughter. Her clothes were unruffled by her effortless hike across the field. She showed no sign of weariness.

Eve caught a waft of her cheap perfume.

Eve, Mum said. *Sweetheart, don't upset the balance love, don't break things.*

And she was light and shade, an illusion of branches and space. Not there, yet…

There.

Eve staggered, back. The apparition, the hallucination, ghost or demon had spoken to her. She couldn't bear this. She couldn't –

Suddenly terrified, she spun about and ran. She had to get away. This was wrong. A deception put there by the Enemy. She gasped for breath, stumbled and tripped. She fell again and again, but each time managed to haul herself up and onto her feet.

Halfway across the field, she stopped to look back.

There was nothing to see but the trees, the acres of churned brown earth and the azure dome of the sky. Nothing. But Eve could feel her, a presence, a shape in the air.

No, this was a temptation. This was an attack, by Satan him…*it*self. This was a sword thrust into an already open wound. This was her forty days in the wilderness. Something was being offered to her but in exchange for what? Her soul? She was stunned. She was under a visible, real, flesh-and-blood supernatural assault. She would fight. She had fought before. She had fought hard, against grief, depression.

And drink.

The minutes passed. Mum did not emerge from the trees. Eve was not sure whether she was disappointed or relieved. She gathered herself together and continued her trek home across the field. Without thinking, she found herself heading for the church rather than the cottage. She needed to pray, and where better than in the House of God.

She was hit with that familiar musty, wood-polish meld of odours when she stepped inside. It was a comforting church smell and churches were her natural habitat. The peace in here was different to the silence outside. The peace in here was profound. It was sacred. She walked up the aisle to kneel a few feet back from the altar, which sat below the huge nave window with its enigmatic image.

Eyes closed, hands clasped, Eve bowed her head and waited a moment before speaking. She was conscious of the window. She wanted to look up and stare at it. She wanted to be drawn into it but resisted. She needed no distraction. She needed only the beat of her own heart and the song of blood as it rushed through her head. She needed to let herself fall into the darkness.

She needed –

The presence was, once again, shocking. She reeled as she was enfolded into the vastness of it. God was here. She was in His arms. She tried to pray and put into words what she felt, her fear, her needs, but there was no point. He was here, a huge weight that bore down on her, an electric charge that shivered through her flesh.

This was her reward. She had kept her faith, oh how she had kept it, despite the awfulness. And now she was a favoured child.

She laughed and threw back her head and absorbed the warmth and the reassurance. Then opened her eyes and the window was once more aglow. This time she was able to hold its glare. This time she saw the blaze of light and colour. Eve felt herself weaken and didn't care. She let herself fall. Because there, at the far end –

Dizzy, she grabbed at her chest and the wildly beating heart it contained until the sensation faded and she was able to breathe again.

*

"Eve?"

"Hello Angela."

The call came in on the rectory's landline. There was still no mobile phone signal.

"Are you all right, Eve? You sound a bit…"

"I'm fine." She wasn't. She was frightened and alone. She had chased an apparition. She had been deafened by God's voice in the church. She was trembling, barely able to think two thoughts in a row and had imprisoned herself in the cottage until she finished her second sermon. She was afraid to go back into the church. Her church. The church in which she would have to preach in a few days' time. She glanced out of the window and out across the field. She was looking for Mum.

"Are you sure?" Angela sounded sceptical.

Eve nodded, which was a foolish gesture when speaking to someone on the telephone. "I'm sure."

"I've an apology to make. I forgot to mention that the congregation hold a house meeting on Wednesday evenings. At the rectory. I'm so sorry to drop this on you like this."

"No, please, It's all right. I'd love to meet some of my flock." Flock? How corny that sounded now, how patronising and parochial. "What sort of thing do you do? What should I prepare?"

"Don't worry, I'll take the meeting. I'll bring some nibbles as well. It's my fault, I didn't warn you. I'll deal with it. We start at about seven-thirty."

"Thanks. I appreciate it."

"No, thank *you*, Eve, for being so understanding."

The connection was cut. Eve sat back in the chair. This was good. Something to look forward to. It would ground her. Meeting other people would snap her out of the madness.

And the need for a drink was growing by the hour. Thank God there was no alcohol in the house.

Chapter Four: House Group

She drank.

A little at first. Just enough to unwind her at the end of the day as she sat in her tiny church-owned, London flat, surrounded by shelves of books and slumped on her tatty sofa. She couldn't remember when it started.

A glass of wine. A gin and tonic. One every evening. Two every evening. It helped. It put the world into soft focus. It blurred its edges and blunted her emotion. It made her light and it made her laugh. She had never been against alcohol, through her time as a lay preacher, the spells in the seminary. Never to excess, wine with a meal, a social drink in a pub with friends. Biblical characters drank. The grand reunion between Joseph and his brothers resulted in them all being "merry". Wasn't that the term used? So why shouldn't she? And then there was the wedding in Cana, water into wine and all the rest.

But this drinking was serious drinking. The merriment it gave her was short lived and rode in on a wave of self-pity and self-disgust. She knew she should stop before an evening pick-me-up became life-support.

She drank because of Leanne. There, in her flat, hunched over, blood dripping from her nose which had been broken by her boyfriend. Leanne who trembled and hugged herself. and dragged her head up so that she could look directly into Eve's eyes and say: "Help me."

She drank because of Nathan, back on the street in the dark, walking with deliberate, teasing slowness to the waiting car. The car which puffed exhaust into the darkness reddened by its taillights. There would be a man inside. A big man. A violent man who held a wad of notes in his hand. Nathan would lean into the open window, talking quietly, coquettish. In for another beating and rape. How else could he make a living and feed his habit? "I like you Lady Rev," he would tell her. "But your God ain't about to send down a consignment of the good stuff, is He? I can't live wivvout the good stuff."

She drank because of Pauline, shivering in her flat, no money, no heat. Her ancient bones were fragile. She was lonely. God, so unutterably lonely. "If it wasn't for you coming to see me every week Lady Rev, I wouldn't see no one at all."

She drank because of the children, innocents, already corrupted by poverty and absence of hope. The little ones were the hardest to bear. The ones who were her when the Shouting People took Mum away.

Then, a week before That Sunday, the Sunday Ruth came to her church, she broke down and cried in the street. She cried for Mum. The grief tore through her like a wave. It was as if the darkness that had been steadily gathering deep in her soul could be contained no longer.

Eve slumped against the glass front of the newsagents where she bought milk and bread. She held herself tightly and gave in. Within moments she felt a hand on her shoulder. A middle-aged woman, her face a mask of concern.

"Why you cryin', love," she said, her West Indian accent strong and soft. Eve recognised her but at that moment, couldn't remember the woman's name. "Reverend, come on, inside. We'll get you a nice cup of tea."

Eve couldn't resist. She allowed the woman, Suzanna that was her name, to take her arm and gently but firmly help her into the shop. A chair appeared. More concerned faces. A mug of sweet tea.

"You been workin' too hard, love," Suzanna told her, now crouched beside her chair, her hand on Eve's. The contact was comforting. "Looking after all of us and not after yourself."

I'm not really caring for you, she answered silently. I'm looking for Mum.

As she sipped hot sweet tea and allowed others to fuss over her, she understood, for the first time, what she was doing. Mum was dead, taken by an overdose in some filthy smack den when Eve was eleven and living a stable, happy life with New Mum and Dad. Eve had been too young to know how to find her mother and had been deprived of her flawed but genuine love by the Court. The news had broken Eve's heart. She had taken to her room for two weeks. Her adopted parents had been patient, kind and strong for her. They had done their best to put her back together.

Mum was dead, but, at the same time, she was still here in this broken community. Reincarnated a thousand times in a thousand blocks of flats and cramped terrace houses. Snorting up lines of white powder, injecting happiness into her veins and paying for it, and for the bare necessities of life, with her own body. Mum, living out her crumbling, meaningless existence over and over again, unheeded and alone, her children loved, but neglected, damaged.

And forsaken.

You left me Mum. You let them take you away and left me on my own.

Eve drank the tea and, as its sweet warmth flowed into her, set about pulling herself together. She couldn't break, she mustn't. She had to keep going.

*

Angela arrived at six, ahead of the rest of the group. She carried a pair of bags filled with crisps, nuts and two tins that contained cakes she had made. She also brought soft drinks and milk for tea and coffee. Eve had prepared a table in the corner of the sitting room and made sure the fire was alight. Lighting it was a minor triumph and made her feel a lot better than she had since her pursuit of Mum's ghost, or whatever that hallucination had been.

The house group members all arrived at the same time, which was either coincidence or superb planning. Whichever it was, their punctuality and co-ordination was disconcerting. Eve heard cars, doors shutting, then a knock. For a moment she was nervous of meeting these people. When she greeted them and invited them in, she realised that there was nothing to fear.

There were seven of them, a wind-torn, rain-damp bunch aged between early twenties and eighty. As well as food and drink, Angela had also brought a handful of fold-up picnic chairs. Eve fetched the study chair from upstairs. Only one person had to sit on the floor, the husband of a serious looking couple in their thirties. The woman, introduced as Zoe, was slim, and fragile-looking. Her hair was tied tightly back from her pale face, which gave her a brittle, nervous air. Her husband, Martin, sported a beard and a shock of curly brown hair. He wore glasses, all of which combined to paint a portrait of a stereotypical academic.

The oldest member of the group was Vivian. She was sprightly, bright-eyed and possessed of a warm, engaging smile. Eve sensed, however that there was a sharp edge hidden beneath the nice-old-lady softness. David and Sandra were a conventional-looking couple in their sixties, he a recently retired bank manager and she the assistant head of a local primary school.

There were two singles, other than Vivian. Nicholas (not Nick), a skinny tall, and slightly nervous young man of around twenty and a pretty, dark-haired and perfectly freckled young woman, named Laura. They were both of a similar age, but there was no obvious chemistry between them.

Angela started with a prayer. Eve bowed her head but was afraid to close her eyes. She felt that she couldn't risk the shock of another face-to-face encounter with God in front of these people, at least, not so early in their acquaintance. At best they would judge her to be a Charismatic, at worst, unhinged. Instead, she stared at the worn carpet between her feet and willed the sledgehammer presence not to bear down on her. She silently asked Him to keep his distance until later, when, she could venture into the white-hot light in the safety of her private devotions.

Angela's prayer was quiet, almost a whisper, yet her words were clear. She seemed intimate with God and much of her conversation with the Almighty consisted of requests for His aid and blessing upon Eve. Eve relaxed. She felt cared for. There was comfort in the warmth of the cottage, the muted rage of the newly-ignited storm outside, the quiet, cadence of Angela's voice and the presence of these other, kindly souls.

The others. The House Group.

The glowing, beautiful-yet-terrible beings in the room.

She started.

Looked up.

The room came back into focus. She blinked. The prayer finished and everyone opened their eyes. There were no beautiful beings. There never had been.

She had seen them. They had frightened her. *Something* had frightened her…

Angela picked up her bible and said, "Ephesians 6; the war between the powers of the air and the armour and weapons of the Christian."

She read the passage. Again, her voice was soft, deep, and almost hypnotic. After a few sentences, Eve was disconcerted to realise that Angela was not actually reading at all but quoting the passage verbatim. Her focus was not on the page, but on Eve, who held her stare and realised that Angela was speaking to her.

"There is a war," Angela said when she had finished her reading. "It is ancient and fierce. It began with conceit, when a powerful angel declared itself as great as God Himself and now all is weighed in the balance of this one conflict."

Eve was startled by the authority in Angela's tone and

something else, behind her words. Something that disturbed her even more. It was a hint of first-hand knowledge. Yes, the believer did experience this fight in the form of their day-to-day struggle, but the experience that lay at the heart of Angela's words seemed different. It was deeper. It was the voice of a veteran who was *there*.

Eve brought herself up short. It was the heat in this room. It was the strain of meeting her new congregation for the first time. It was this new responsibility and the loneliness that went with it –

The memory of last night returned. The hallucination she had experienced in the church. The figure that emerged from the blaze of light in the stained-glass window. An angel. Angel. Angela…

Stop it.

Eve forced her attention back to the moment.

"…armies, angels engaged in eternal battle. Locked in catastrophic struggle that destroys stars and sends galaxies spinning off their axis. Wars that rage within the hearts of fiery nebulae, and shatter planets into dust. It is a balance, a stalemate. But…" She scanned the room. The atmosphere, already taut, tightened further. "There is the possibility of victory. We have the means, the one who will open the door to those who would change sides, those who would cast off the soiled rags of obedience to Lucifer and don the pure armour of God. Who will release these prisoners?" And now her eye was fixed squarely on Eve.

"Jesus," Eve murmured. Speech was suddenly difficult, as if the words were tangled in her throat. "He will release…"

No one should. Mum. It was Mum. The shock of her voice,

her whisper close to her ear, caused Eve to break the contact and look wildly around the room. She caught a glimpse, a shadow, a brief, movement, shape and presence.

That cheap perfume.

Not even you, sweetheart.

Then it was gone.

"Mum?"

Silence fell, suddenly. Eve was appalled to realise that she had spoken the name out loud. She looked round at the others. "Sorry, I…"

There were changes in the room, shadows that did not reflect their owners but were vast and inhuman. Something shone through the faces of the people sitting in her lounge. She heard a voice…voices, their voices…a command, a whisper that was like clashing steel. "Go."

Mum cried out, as if in pain. The sound flared loud in Eve's head then faded as if she was falling away. The perfume scent faded with her cry. Eve surged to her feet. She wanted her back. She wanted to reach into the darkness and grasp Mum's hand and save her.

"Eve?"

She started and there was Angela, concerned, leaning forward in her chair. "You zoned out for a moment."

"I thought I heard…It's hot in here."

She glanced at the others. They sat in the same chairs and in the same attitudes as before. Most smiled a reassuring smile. Vivian remained serious. "Don't believe her," she said quietly. "That isn't your mother. It's a trick, a deceit. It's frightened. It will do anything to save itself."

"Who?" Eve asked. She was still on her feet. She felt

awkward, self-conscious but she could not let this go. "What's frightened?"

Vivian smiled her kindly smile. "Sorry?" Her voice was the quivery tone of a slightly confused elderly lady. "What do you mean, frightened?"

The sudden transformation angered Eve. She was being played, but discretion, she decided, was the better part of valour at this moment. She was at a disadvantage. She had little idea of what was happening.

"Let's finish up now," Angela said. "I'll get you a cold drink."

"Good idea." Eve made to follow Angela to the kitchen. Vivian was on her feet in an instant. She put a gnarled old hand on Eve's shoulder. "You stay right where you are, dear. Sit down. You look a little pale and shaken-up. It's all a bit strange for you at the moment. We understand. It will take you a little while to find your feet."

"Especially coming from London to a remote spot like this," the fragile-looking Laura added. "You know we really do appreciate this."

"Yes," Vivian said. "We really do need someone like you to take care of us."

"Someone like me?" Eve asked.

"Yes," Laura said. "You have a deep, *real* faith. You have a tangible relationship with God."

"How do you know this?" Eve was aware that the statement was delivered sharply and was embarrassed, although why should she be? These people were making a lot of assumptions about her.

Neither Vivian nor Laura recoiled from her question. "We

are aware of what happened in London," Vivian said. "We know the choice you made and how it broke you, but through it all, you continued to seek the face of God, even though you were angry, even though your heart was in pieces –"

Unable to bear their attention any longer, Eve got to her feet. "Please stop, I don't want to talk about this."

Again, those understanding smiles that unnerved rather than comforted. Eve forced herself to calm down. "Look, I appreciate your sentiments and understanding. I really do. I appreciate that you do not judge me. But I need to put the past behind me. I need to serve you here to the best of my ability. Please, let's start from scratch, with a clean slate."

"Of course," said David the retired bank manager. "We're sorry. I suppose we're all a little excited to have such a church celebrity as our shepherd. The work you did in that London parish, amazing."

Celebrity?

"Thank you."

"We're sorry," Sandra, said. "We didn't mean to open old wounds."

Yes, you did, Eve told her silently. "I'm looking forward to getting to know you all and working for God in this parish."

Who are you? Eve asked them silently. Then chided herself that she was being foolish. They were members of her, no doubt small, congregation. They were a tight-knit community comfortable in each other's company and able to speak their minds. It was always hard to be a newcomer in such a long-standing group. It was going to take time.

There was a murmur of conversation now. The spell was broken.

"And as for being a celebrity," Eve said, "does that mean I'll have to wear a headscarf and dark glasses when I go into the village?"

A poor joke, but enough. There was laughter. Tension broken.

Mum was outside.

Eve could feel her presence. She could see her in her mind's eye, standing on the driveway, on the far side of the parked cars. The wind plucked at her tangled hair and scoured her face. Eve wanted to rush over to the window, wrench back the curtains and look. She wanted to fling open the door and let her in.

Let her *back* in.

Because she was here before and it had unsettled the house group as much as it had unsettled Eve.

No. Vivian had been right. This Mum who was haunting her was a trick, a deceit perpetrated by someone who was frightened.

The conversation flowed. There was laughter, the glow of new friends. Eve should have been at ease, but she wasn't. There was something wrong. These people. They seemed normal enough, the type of people she would have expected to be part of a church house group. And that was the point. It was as if they had stepped out of her mind, fully formed. Seven stereotypes.

She was, of course, imagining what wasn't there. For every strange occurrence so far, there was a logical explanation. She needed to relax. These people were on her side. There was no Mum, not anymore. Eve did her best, chatted and circulated and picked at the snacks. All home-cooked by the look and taste of them, a delight of flavours, savoury and sweet, few of them familiar.

Then, after about two hours, the group members began get to their feet and make their goodbyes. They left as they had arrived, all at once and quickly. Except for Angela, who Eve had always known was going to stay behind.

The pair of them cleared-up and washed the dishes in companionable silence. The quiet let in the storm.

"Coffee?" Eve said when she and Angela had finished.

"If you don't mind."

"I need the company."

"So, do I if the truth be known," Angela said.

"I wouldn't have said you were a lonely person."

Angela didn't answer straight away. She stood over the sink and stared at the window. The blind covered the storm and the view, but Eve had a sense that Angela could see out anyway. "I'm more alone than you can ever imagine."

"What do you mean?"

"Nothing –"

"Angela, I'm tired of evasion. That meeting tonight, it was…it wasn't what it seemed. It was…"

"What was it? Be honest with me."

"It was fake." Eve tensed, waiting for a backlash, or at least an offended protest.

Instead, Angela smiled. "No, not fake. Those people are real enough. And we do meet once a week, we need each other. We are a bastion. We are an outpost in the war."

"Anyone living the Christian life is living in an outpost."

"True. But you can't possibly understand what this place is."

"It's what happens at any given moment that makes a place

ᵧₐₙₐ s smile widened. "The way you made St Martin's sacred, by your good works and faithfulness?"

"Please, I made nothing holy or sacred. I don't like people telling me that I did. You know as well as I do that Jesus said that if a man asks for a cloak, give him your coat —"

Without warning, Angela's hand closed about Eve's. She tensed, unsure of whether she wanted this.

"Vivian was right. It isn't your mother," Angela said.

"What do you mean?"

"The apparition you've been seeing, it isn't really Caroline Clement."

Eve flinched back, too startled to offer a denial. "How do you know I've seen her?"

"You spoke her name tonight, at the meeting."

"Yes, but…"

"It's a deception."

"I know. I've never lived alone like this before. There's no one or anything for miles and miles. It's hardly surprising that I'm seeing ghosts."

"It's trying to trick you, Eve."

"What is?"

"Lucifer, it's afraid of this place and afraid of you. It tried to bring you down once before, didn't it? But it failed. You remained faithful. Now, it's attacking you again, where you're most vulnerable. I'm here to look out for you." Angela's arm went about her shoulder. Eve gave in and leaned against the woman and let the comfort of it take her. She felt too tired and weak to fight.

Chapter Five: The Walk

It was just after noon on Friday when Eve set out for the village. The sky was a clear azure dome. The air was fresh and the sun, though pale and devoid of heat, added to Eve's good feeling. She walked at a brisk pace. There was plenty to feel good about. She was again close to God, in fact, she felt closer to Him than she had ever been. It would take time for her to grow accustomed to the sheer volume and brightness of it when she prayed, but He was there, looking after her.

Yesterday had been a trial. But she had gritted her teeth and managed to stay in and around the rectory and rough out two sermons for Sunday. She had walked the fields to the copse then beyond until she was exhausted. Loneliness was the worst part of it. The temptation to phone Angela had been overwhelming. Her absence had allowed Eve's thoughts to boil over. Old emotions and griefs had fought their way to the surface. She let them come. She let them darken the blue sky and beat her into submission. She was too tired to fight and unsure how.

The evening storm had been welcome.

No more silence. No more stillness. Now there was noise

and movement, physicality and violence. The rectory had gone from being a prison to a refuge.

The storm had been her lullaby. She slept well.

When she woke, she felt refreshed and happier. She was where she was supposed to be and that was all that mattered. For the first time since she had lost Ruth, Eve was at peace. She strode along the narrow lane, now between high, leafless hedgerows, now passing acres of lonely brown fields, dotted with more of those miniature woods. Two miles, wasn't that what Angela had said? She must have covered that distance by now, yet there was no sign of any houses, no evidence, in fact, that the village of Weddon actually existed at all.

Country miles must be longer than town ones, she mused and pressed on.

Lovely as this was, it emphasised the point that she really did need a car.

For the first time she relished the loneliness. She needed it. She needed to fight her battles undisturbed and undistracted. There would be a battle. She was certain of that. A battle not easily won.

And then there was Ruth…

…They were back at Eve's flat.

She couldn't remember when they agreed to do this. Ruth had simply called her on her mobile one night and told her she wanted to meet for a coffee. It seemed natural. Eve tried to convince herself that Ruth wanted to discuss some community project with her, but she couldn't dampen the frisson of excitement the invitation brought. Ruth had been on her mind since their meeting outside the church three

Sundays ago. She had returned the following Sunday evening and waited around until the congregation had dispersed. Then she sat with Eve in the church and talked for an hour about her hopes for the constituency and her plans and campaign. The air between them tightened. There were overlong glances. There was…electricity.

Yes, Ruth had wanted to talk over a community centre project Eve was working towards, but it was a thinly veiled excuse. They ended up back at Eve's flat. Ruth sat on the sofa, both hands curled tightly about a mug of coffee. She was suddenly awkward, shy, almost. Eve sat at her desk; office chair swivelled about to face her.

"You're a good person," Ruth said quietly.

"So are you." The complements held a surprisingly erotic charge.

"Am I?" Ruth chuckled ruefully. "I'm married and I'm making a mess of that and I'm lonely."

Some force pushed Eve up onto her feet. It was impossible for her to understand what that force was except that it was not to be resisted. She was being foolish; she shouldn't be crossing the short distance to the sofa. Ruth should stand, shake her head and say "No, Eve, this is wrong." She should tell Ruth to go. But here she was, standing in front of her and reaching out. Her arm, her hand, all operated by some energy she could not control and yet had full control over. There was no logic here, or morals or sense. She was trembling. She felt a little panic. She wanted it to stop, but at the same time did not want it to ever stop.

Ruth looked up at her and, as she did so, the voice of sanity in Eve's mind, the voice of conscience and of God faded into confusion. Ruth stood and her arms slid about Eve's shoulders and she pulled her into a kiss. It was natural and easy. Eve had no conscience in that moment. She had no God or even self.

This was inevitable, wasn't it? This meeting of flesh on a sultry, storm-laden evening. Lightning flashed with suitable drama through the open window. Thunder rolled and echoed over the city.

Later, in Eve's bed, entwined and at peace, she wondered what God saw as He gazed down at her. Was He angry? Was this an abomination, this moment of soft, sweet joy?

"You really are a sinner now," Ruth said and for one disconcerting, crazy moment Eve wondered if the woman had read her mind, or if she was some infernal succubus, perhaps even the Devil herself.

"A sinner? I suppose I am," Eve answered, and the dark thought dissolved. She chuckled. "I've certainly proved the Bishop and his cabal right. An unsuitable woman who not only doesn't know her place but engages in lustful pursuits of the most depraved kind."

"Is that how you see this?"

"No, of course not…"

"You don't seem too sure." There was no accusation in Ruth's voice. She was propped on her right elbow, looking down at Eve. Ruth was an indistinct shape in the gloom, briefly lit by a bright stab of lightning that sliced into the room.

"I…I don't see this as wrong, but…the Bible…I've never…"

"Eve, do you believe in a celibate priesthood?"

"I'm an Anglican, we don't –"

"No, listen to me. Do you believe in a celibate priesthood?"

"No."

"Do you have a liking for choirboys or little girls?"

"Of course not, Ruth, don't say that –"

"Are you lonely?"

"Not at this moment, but, well, yes. I am lonely."

"There are a lot of single, attractive men out there."

"I'm not interested. Look, Ruth, the Bible is a little tough on, well, you know…"

"On two people of the same sex falling in love and finding comfort and peace with each other? Yes, I'm aware of what certain, obscure parts of the Good Book have to say on the matter. It also says that we shouldn't wear certain mixes of material or have battlements on our houses. And that Saint Paul, what a great chap he was, he sent a slave back to his owner and he told women to keep their mouths shut in church. I think there's a bit of cherry picking going on here, don't you? Sins graded by prejudice?"

Eve had no answer.

"Eve? Are you okay with this? I need to know."

"Yes."

A pause. "You're breaking yourself."

"What do you mean?"

"You're killing yourself, Eve. You're working yourself to death."

"It's Mum." The words slipped out, unbidden.

Eve sensed Ruth's puzzlement.

"She was arrested when I was a child. I feel…I feel as if I should have saved her."

"That's ridiculous."

"I know," Eve said. "I was seven. I was…"

"Scared?" Ruth drew her close. "It must have been horrible."

"No. No I wasn't frightened. I was confused, numb. I remember it clearly. I think a part of me understood what was happening."

"Even so, you were a child –"

"I know the logic of it, but this isn't about logic."

"So now you're trying to save her all over again, is that it?" Ruth nuzzled her hair. Eve closed her eyes and silently begged for time to stand still. She allowed the other woman to hold her and to be childlike. "None of this is about logic."

A sigh. "It's getting late. I'd better –"

"Don't go," Eve whispered.

This was no longer a joke. This was no longer pleasant. According to the time on her mobile phone, Eve had been walking for over an hour now. There had been no side road, turnings or junctions, just this endless lane with its alternating hedgerows and views across the countryside. Uneasy and irritated, she began to wonder if the views were the same ones each time and that the passing landscape was like the repetitive backdrops used in cartoons. The thought was maddening. She was walking. Her feet were moving her along the road. But she was getting nowhere and to add to her unease, the gaps in the hedge revealed cloud, building on the horizon. The air was colder, the light losing its clarity.

A breeze troubled the air. Cloud edged into the strip of sky that roofed the gap between the tops of the hedgerows. She felt rain.

The breeze strengthened.

She stopped walking. She was frustrated by her inability to find the village. She was angry at Angela for giving her false instructions. And she was frightened. She was alone out here, and the storm was closing in. There was no choice, was there? She had to turn back.

A part of her, the stubborn, determined part of her wanted to her to keep walking and somehow defeat this ridiculous, infuriating emptiness and find that fucking village – oh yes, she was that angry. But the sensible part of her, her head, she supposed, knew that it would be a fruitless search. She had made a mistake somewhere –

But where? There had been no other roads, she was certain of it.

The first drops of the rain stung her face.

She turned back.

Now the walk was an endurance test. The wind brought with it the lash of rain. She was exhausted. She was cold. The hedgerow hissed and creaked on either side and any glimpses of countryside it allowed her were obscured by a wall of rain.

This wasn't English rain, was it? This was a monsoon. She forced herself on, head down, the rain hammered at her hood. Drenched the legs of her jeans. The parka was waterproof, but heavy now with moisture.

Wind howled down the narrow funnel that was the lane. It brought wave upon wave of rain that felt as if it was made from broken glass. She pressed on. Her anger gave her energy.

And there was the church and the rectory, much closer than it should be. She had walked further than this on the outward journey. She had walked for an hour. But she was home. There could be no disputing the fact.

She should be glad of it. She needed to get inside to warm up and dry out.

Especially as the light was fading fast, which was as strange as the suddenness with which she had found herself at home. It was as if the day had telescoped. She fumbled the key and all but fell inside. Clothes off, shower then a thick, soft arran-knit and PJ pants instead. Fresh clothes. When she had finished and was brushing her hair, she noticed the time on her phone. Five-thirty.

Impossible.

She sighed and carried on tearing through the wet tangles in her sodden hair.

Finished, dry and warm, she made coffee and sat down by the fireplace. She would try to light it, but the coffee came first. As she drank, she realised that she was angry with Angela, as if it was the Deacon's fault that she had been beaten back by the storm. And as for the village being only a couple of miles away. That wasn't Angela's fault either, but Eve found it hard to convince herself of the fact. The Deacon had been nothing but loyal, welcoming and faithful.

She had also lied.

There was also that bizarre compression of time. Eve had no explanation for that, other than disorientation caused by the storm. She was exhausted. It felt like the evening. It felt as if an entire afternoon had passed unnoticed.

It had.

Coffee drunk, she lit the fire and was pleasantly surprised that her fire-starting skills were improving with each attempt –

This place was wrong.

The realisation didn't so much hit her as unfolded itself in her mind. This place was off kilter. She felt the beginnings of panic. She was trapped here. Whichever way she walked, it would lead her deeper into never-ending countryside.

Impossible, of course. Hadn't she arrived at a railway station and been driven here by Angela? And where had the church group come from?

Thunder rumbled outside. Eve closed her eyes. The sound was threatening tonight. It bore down on her as it broke through the howl of the wind and the relentless beat of rain on the window. Hugging herself, Eve got to her feet and crossed the room, intent on closing the curtains. She would pray. She would face the noise and light head-on.

She didn't want to. She wanted to curl up on the chair by the fire, close her eyes and escape into sleep.

Eve reached the window and peered out. She expected to see Mum out there.

Her breath caught in her throat. She rushed out into the hall to grab her coat and wrench open the front door for a better view. No, not view, but confirmation that she had seen what she thought she had seen. She stood in the doorway, looked up and stared at the storm-torn night sky.

A battle raged up there. A titanic struggle between armies of giants that surged about the canyons of lightning-flamed clouds. Glimpsed then lost in the darkness, although never fully gone because the light of it seeped from the edges of the roiling cloud and turned the rain gold as it fell. Another lightning flash and she saw it again, human-like monsters, locked in struggle, great sprays of electricity where hands clasped about arms, vast faces twisted into masks of effort…

…armies, angels engaged in eternal battle. Locked in catastrophic struggle that destroys stars and sends galaxies spinning off their axis. Wars that rage within the hearts of fiery nebulae, and shatter planets into dust. It is a balance, a stalemate.

A blast of wind drove her back. Thunder rolled across the glowing translucent sky. Only it wasn't thunder. It was the sound of war.

She stumbled back and slammed the door shut behind her. The door shuddered under the impact of a fist. Or a boot. Or a battering ram. The Shouting People were back.

Mum! Mum, wake up and run

Now it was the windows. The walls. Someone out there who wanted to get in. The pounding became a staccato, machine-gun madness. Eve closed her eyes tight. She put her hands over her ears and slid onto her knees.

"God," she cried out. "God, where are you?"

Here.

That nearness, that brutal presence. She recoiled but fought to hold on.

"I need you. Help me. Please protect me. I'm sorry. I'm sorry…"

The darkness behind her eyes flared with light every bit as bright as the lightning outside and deep in the darkness Eve saw a figure. It was incomprehensible. It was a terror and a joy. It was ancient and *all and everything*.

And close. So close.

Eve felt herself fall into the light. She wanted to give in. She wanted its embrace.

"Help me…"

The light and sound of it, of *Him*, flared and was

unbearable, yet she clung on. All trouble and grief fled from her. She was gripped with an ecstasy that was almost orgasmic. She wanted to fall deeper. She wanted to stay. This was life. Everything else was death. This was reality. This was home. She cried out and fell back and opened her eyes. She woke, lying on the floor and shivered despite the warmth of the fire she had lit.

The wrench from the divine to the carnal left her sobbing with grief. She couldn't help it. Again, she had been offered love and warmth and again it had been torn from her grasp.

The sense of loss began to fade, but it left a vast emptiness within her. She lay, wide-eyed, imagining the titanic battle in the skies above her. No longer afraid of whatever was pounding at the doors and windows.

Soon, there was no sound but the storm.

And then a dream that was a memory…

"I'm puzzled," Ruth said.

It was late September, Sunday night and dark. London was a dull backdrop roar punctuated by the noise of the non-stop traffic immediately outside the flat. Eve was sleepy, her hand curled about Ruth's. They were too weary to make love, content, rather, to lie side-by-side. Comforted and contented by each other's presence.

"Mmm?" Eve said.

"I said, I don't get that passage you read in church this evening, the one about Job."

"'The one about Job'? You make it sound like a joke."

"A joke? Oh yeah, you know the one. There was this god, see, and one day the Devil came to visit him and said, 'That

Job, all he's giving you is cupboard love."'

"Hey, come on, that's a bit disrespectful." Eve wasn't being entirely flippant. She loved God, but there was a healthy dose of fear mixed in. God, the Bible said, was a consuming fire. She had certainly been burned during her thirty-or-so years. She had seen the flames and she had felt the fragility of the ground on which she stood.

And wasn't she dancing close to those flames again? Right here and now, in this bed? She trusted that God understood and wasn't angry with her over this. She believed that He wanted her to be happy, but there was a price; respect and devotion to Him. One sin could be allowed providing there were no others. A deal. A bargain.

Except that it was in her head, surely. You didn't make deals with Him. Her peace of mind was an act of will, not of faith. On the other hand, there had, so far, been no divine punishment, no lightning strike or heart attack.

"You started it."

"I know I did, and I shouldn't have."

"Sorry," Ruth said. "I was being disrespectful."

"It's okay. I'm sure God is big enough to take a little ribbing now and then." Careful. God might be long-suffering, but His patience had limits.

Ruth rolled over. She was close. Eve breathed in her scent, that meld of perfume, sweat and the musk of sex. She wanted Ruth to kiss her. Instead, Ruth said; "I thought Satan had been cast out of Heaven."

"He was."

"Well, suddenly he's back and not only that, he's challenging God face-to-face, marching up and down in front of Him and taunting Him over one of His faithful."

"I don't think it's meant to be taken literally –"

"Even if it isn't, it's still an odd scenario."

"Perhaps, but to me the whole story is about faithfulness through trial."

"I understand that, but something doesn't add up."

Ruth was right, it didn't.

"Are you calling my sermon into question?"

"It was a good sermon."

"Oh, I bet you say that to all the lady vicars you bed."

"It never fails."

"Well, what do you want me to do with this theological enigma?" Eve said.

"Store it away, you might need it one day."

Ruth was close now. Eve felt her gentle and sweet-scented breath on her lips. Suddenly she was no longer tired. Her desire unfolded as it always did when Ruth kissed her like that, and with it, the sadness and the guilt.

I'm going to lose you, she told her silently. Oh God, Ruth, I am going to lose you.

Chapter Six: The Death Of Nathan Steel

Perhaps it started with the death of Nathan Steel.

"You need to step back a little," Bishop Paul said to her two weeks after Eve and Ruth had made love for the first time. For one panicked moment, Eve thought that he had found out about them, but then he added; "That parish will break you if you get too involved with its people." There was steel under his sympathetic tone.

"Isn't that my job?" Eve was in the office in the Bishop's residence. Office was probably too strong a word for the slightly shabby comfort of the bookcase-lined room. He poured her a brandy then leaned against his enormous oak desk, buttocks resting against its routed edge. Eve sat in one of the armchairs. "These people need someone who isn't a policeman or social worker or from an official body –"

"The church is primarily concerned with the spiritual needs of its flock. Yes, of course we offer support and comfort where we can, but we are not social workers." Paul's sympathetic tone deepened. "You look tired, Eve. I'm worried about you. I heard about your…upset, in the town a few weeks ago. That's why I've taken a personal interest."

"I appreciate your concern –"

"There's also your close association with Ruth Chandler."

The panic returned. "What about her?"

Here it came. The storm breaking. The world ending. The ultimatum.

"She is the Labour candidate in the forthcoming election. A politician. Church and politics Eve, not a good combination. Even Jesus said so; render unto Caesar what is Caesar's and to God, what is God's."

"Aren't Bishops members of the House of Lords?" Eve said.

"Yes, but we're neutral."

"So am I. I have friends and acquaintances from all sides and opinions. Ruth is just another of those friends. It just so happens that she is someone who wants to get her hands dirty and help the people in that borough. Her political colours mean nothing to me."

Paul looked sceptical but didn't comment. Instead, he said; "You're involved with Vicky Steel's campaign."

"She's just lost her son to knife crime and she is talking publicly about it and doing something to raise awareness of the problem. She's in my parish. She has asked me for help."

"I understand. Difficult not to. A bright student knifed to death by a bunch of thugs," Paul said. Such an old-fashioned word, thugs. "But also, it turns out, a drug dealer."

"A lot of the kids make money selling weed," Eve countered. "We treat teenagers like kids and won't let them work until they're eighteen. No wonder they grab an opportunity when it's offered to them."

"You're not condoning –"

"Of course, I'm not." She knew that she was being somewhat disrespectful, but she couldn't help herself. It wasn't the first time they had crossed swords. She was, she knew, a troublesome priest. "I'm providing pastoral care to the family."

"Well, you're sailing a bit too close to politics here, Eve. You have to stay neutral and you have to back away."

How could she? Vicky Steel, single mum, helpless in Eve's arms. Her weeping was the raw cry of a wounded animal. She loved her son, despite his failings and his choice of casual labour. Vicky was a woman who had lost her child and who clung to Eve after the cremation because she had no strength to stand or breathe on her own.

"Please help us," she had said.

The thought of not doing so was alien to Eve. Of course, she would. And she did. For much of the time that help had been simply to visit the woman in her tiny flat, a hundred or so feet above the earth, let her cry and listen to her and pray with her.

Vicky was healing a little now. She had found her strength again, the strength that enabled her to raise three children alone in one of the roughest estates in the borough. Eve admired her. Vicky's other two children, daughters, seemed as strong and well-intentioned as their mother.

Both were working hard to get away from the area. Education was the way out, the older one had said. It would get them good jobs. Money.

"I admire your rapport with the less fortunate of your parish, believe me, I have no second thoughts about that." Paul said. He did have second thoughts, it was writ plain

on his face, in the almost imperceptible strain ⸗
smile, in the hardness of his light brown eyes. He w⸗
uncomfortable with the amount of dirt Eve got on her hands.
"But we have to tread carefully."

"Perhaps that's why most of our churches are half empty."

"What do you mean?"

"Because we always tread carefully and do and say nothing."

"Now. That isn't fair –"

"Vicky Steel needs pastoral care. She's strong but she is also
fragile. She can't afford counselling, she can't afford anything
that might help her, but she can afford me because what we give
is free. The Bible says, 'True religion and undefiled is to comfort
the sick and fatherless.' I think Vicky comes under that clause."

Paul regarded her carefully for a moment. Then said;
"You're a troublemaker, Eve. You always have been." There
was no affection or admiration in his tone. His voice was
hard. "Be careful. We cannot afford another scandal. We have
enough of those as it is. If I see your face on the television,
even in the crowd or walking past in the background, I will be
forced to act. Do you understand?"

She did and the threat, although heavy-handed and reeking
of tough-talking television drama, struck home. This was her
calling. Her reason for living. She could not lose that.

"I'll do my best."

*

Eve stood in the centre of the Emerson, Lake and Palmer
tower blocks once again. She had lost count how many
times she had walked across the scrap of weed and grass

to the graffiti-daubed sculpture that formed the triangle's centrepiece. Again, she wondered which council genius had decided that this odd jumble of shapes somehow represented, or enhanced, the sky-high, piss-reeking, concrete and glass prison blocks they had sanctioned and financed.

There was nothing except a small pile of wilted flowers and weather-worn cards to show that a young human life, had been torn away on this spot. He had bled into this rough, unkempt grass then slipped away to face God. Surely, Eve told herself, and again, not for the first time, He would have mercy on Nathan Steel. Nathan was sixteen. He was young and stupid just as everyone was entitled to be young and stupid at that age.

The press had not been so merciful, of course. All they had to say was that he was a drug dealer. Did a few ounces of weed, sold on a street corner, make him a drug dealer? It didn't seem a great sin in the scheme of things, but it had cost him his life. The people who ran the drug trade were merciless. Nathan must have crossed some line, made some minor mistake. Punishment had been swift and final.

The sun beat down hard on the triangle then, just as Eve reached the spot where a paramedic had fought to save Nathan's life, it faded behind a large, indigo cloud that slid into the three-cornered patch of sky framed by the triple towers. Suddenly cold, Eve hugged herself. The light blouse she wore open and loose over her short-sleeved top and clerical collar, did little to keep out the momentary gust of chill wind the clouds brought with them.

Vicky had seen none of it. Eve studied the Emerson tower, to where she estimated the Steel's window would be, up there, near the summit of the building. To Vicky the sirens and the shouting would have been distant. Just another night's drama somewhere on the estate. A tired ritual that held no interest for her and was no reason to go to her window and look down.

"God bless, Nathan." Eve bowed her head and uttered a short prayer. The cloud moved on and was replaced by heat and brightness. Eve tugged at her clerical collar. It felt hot and restrictive this morning.

She set off towards Emerson.

So far, she had encountered no trouble. She never came here at night, of course; usually, like now, it was around ten in the morning. Most of the troublemakers were nowhere in sight. Still in bed, presumably.

There were good people on this estate. There always were, but the media wasn't interested in good people. Nor were the police.

Inside Emerson, the lift grumbled and groaned its way up to the twelfth floor. It smelled as always of disinfectant and urine. There was a stale alcohol smell in here this morning as well. That made a refreshing change. The doors slid open with alarming slowness and for a moment, Eve wondered if she was going to be trapped in here.

Not today.

There was voice behind Vicky's battered-looking, light-green door. Eve pressed the bell button. Both of the voices were female. A few seconds later she heard footsteps then the door opened.

"Hello Eve."

"Hello Vicky."

A hug. Vicky's hugs were tight and filled with gladness and tears.

"There's someone else here. Someone important," she said as she led Eve into her small, and always immaculate, sitting room. The room was flooded with light from the large window which took up one entire wall and gave a view of the Lake and Palmer towers and the city beyond.

The other guest was Ruth. She wore a suit, looked smart and energised and was quickly on her feet, hand extended in greeting. Her obviously habitual and professional smile softened into delight. Startled, Eve almost hugged her but remembered where she was and the secrecy of their relationship.

"Reverend Clements."

"Ms Chandler."

Ruth held her hand for a moment longer than was normal for a handshake. Eve was surprised by a sudden anger. Why hadn't Ruth told her she was getting involved in this as well?

"I was just telling Vicky that while this is a local issue, it's also a national one," Ruth said. "I want to help."

"Publicity-seeking, in other words."

Ruth flinched but her the smile lost none of its shine. She knew Eve's comment wasn't altogether teasing, but she looked as if she enjoyed it, nonetheless.

"Really?" Ruth said. "So, where is the press? Where are the cameras?"

"Ruth wants to help us, especially the youngsters," Vicky said.

"Vicky —" First name terms already? "— is starting a campaign to get a youth centre built on the estate, and a playground, down there, for the children. She said that you had suggested a day centre where single mothers could meet to talk and be together and swap clothes for their babies and children. It's a fantastic idea. This place lacks a sense of community. The gangs have taken control of it and it's time for the people to take that control back."

"I understand why our kids join gangs," Vicky said. "They want to belong, of course they do, but what if there were other things they could belong to?"

Eve made to speak, but Ruth spoke first. "Your ideas are unfocussed at the moment, Vicky. We need to start with one project, a first step, something I can campaign on and that we can actually achieve."

Vicky nodded. The grief was still etched into the landscape of her open, warm face. There was a brightness there too, her eyes shone. She looked like someone ready for the fight. Perhaps she had found a direction and purpose, a way of making sense of what happened.

"The problem is that it all comes down to money," Ruth said. "The council are strapped for cash. They all are. We need to raise money for this, show a willingness to do it ourselves, and then ask the council and other bodies to match us. We need to go to other parties, businesses, for example, they like the publicity. We could try to crowd fund. If I am elected, I will fight for this."

"And if you're not?" Eve said.

Ruth flinched and this time there was no playful response. This time she looked hurt.

Eve was immediately angry with herself, both for her harshness towards the woman she loved and for her negative stance. She couldn't help it. Ruth had barged in here, like the cavalry. Did she not understand the complexity of the problems that existed in this place? Nonetheless, she was trying to change things for the better. Wasn't that why she loved her? Eve softened her tone when she spoke again. "All right then." Eve said. "I think we should start with the drop-in centre. The closed-down pub behind Palmer Tower would be perfect. A rota can be drawn up of those who run it. I'm sure there will be people at the church who would love to help. It will give some of them a place to go. Especially some of the older and lonely ones. It will give the kids a chance to meet other kids at a young age. It will help struggling young mothers by creating a clothes swap. They could babysit for each other. It will be a start. The problem here, as I see it, is isolation."

"All right, how does that sound, Vicky?" Ruth said.

The light shone even brighter in Vicky's face, but there were tears too. The light was a thin mask and it was cracking already.

"I still want to go out there and talk to those boys," she said. "I'm going to do it, even if I have to do it on my own. I'm going out there on Friday night and I'm going to talk to them and tell them that they are wasting their lives and that they are going to end up in prison."

"I'll be there. I promised I would, and I will," Eve said.

"Me too," Ruth said.

*

They left together. The door to Vicky's flat slammed shut.

"Me too?"

Ruth held Eve's stare. "Yes."

"This isn't a political stunt, you know. We don't want cameras and journalists and –"

"You won't have them. I'll be alone. Why are you angry?" She sounded hurt, which made Eve feel shabby again..

"I…I don't want publicity," Eve said. "I don't want this to be turned into a reality show."

"This? Do you mean Vicky's plan or *this*?"

"Both."

"Thank God for that. I don't think my husband…" Ruth stopped herself. "I'm sorry."

"I know. So am I." Ruth's mention of her husband, Nick, drove guilt straight into Eve's soul. It also brought a wave of hopelessness. Ruth was never going to leave him and if she did there would be an immense scandal replete with tears and pain.

So, what should she do about it? Stupid question. Eve knew exactly what she should do.

Not yet. Not now. This moment was an unexpected one. A chance for time together. She needed to cling to it. Stretch it out.

"Coffee?" Eve said.

"I thought you'd never ask."

They drove their separate cars to the nearest Costa and reconvened at a corner table. Not for discretion, there was one advantage to this type of affair, Eve mused. There was nothing suspicious in two women having a cappuccino together.

The place was relatively empty. They sat by a window. The smell of coffee was another of those good smells Eve loved. She leaned on the table and stared out at the street.

All the usual shops, a constant procession of cars and vans and the occasional lorry. People, all of them in a hurry. The sun, bright, although occasionally dulled by a passing cloud, painted the pavement white.

No one paid them any attention or even recognised Ruth. Unsurprising as politics and its practitioners were mainly ignored in this part of the borough. "Cappuccino for you, Americano for me. And a snack." Ruth placed two packs of assorted nuts on the table. "I can't believe the price of these things." She shook her head then ripped open both packs and helped herself. There was a naturalness to her movement. Even in something as mundane as this. At ease. Graceful.

And all the time, the wedding ring glinted on her finger. A reminder for Eve to rein in her feelings and try to dampen the thrill that this was.

"You've got to believe me," Ruth said. "I'm not doing this for cameras and headlines." She laughed. "I can see scepticism written all over your face, Eve."

"You're a politician, Ruth."

"I am indeed."

"Why were you so keen to help Vicky?" Eve asked after a coffee moment. "I mean, there are plenty of other projects you could have taken part in, safer ones."

Ruth nodded. "I believe in what I'm…what we are doing. I want to help this place."

Eve wanted to ask why but waited. It was obvious that Ruth had more to say but was finding it difficult.

"I…I'm not always this upbeat." she said. There was a brief smile.

"None of us are." Oh God, please stop me trotting out

the platitudes.

"I suffer from depression."

Ah. Eve waited. She fought a new urge, not to simply offer another stock response, but to place her hand on Ruth's.

"Not a good condition for a politician," Ruth sounded close to tears.

"Churchill's black dog didn't stop him."

"No, you're right and that's what I've told myself over and over again. I won't be stopped by this. It comes and goes. Today, this week, this month so far, has been a good one. You, Eve, are a light in the dark." Ruth glanced around then laid her hand on

Eve's. The contact was made tender by the way her hand trembled a little. "I love you."

*

It was eight pm. A week later. Daylight persisted but was beginning to fade. It was hot and Eve was agitated. She had been working on a sermon for most to the day but had been distracted and unable to concentrate.

All the way to the Emerson, Lake and Palmer Towers she had known that she was making a mistake. Her guilt over Ruth and what she was doing to her husband and children would not go away. She was a minister of God. She had responsibilities. She couldn't continue the affair. Wasn't her role to bring peace and goodness, not pain? Yet, the thought of ending this seemed more impossible with each day. Life without Ruth was an absence she could no longer comprehend. It was a waste howling wilderness. It was the equivalent of ripping off one of her limbs.

"Hi," Ruth said. Eve had parked next to her in the area adjacent to the flats and was getting out of her car.

Ruth wore a dark jacket, trousers and an expensive-looking sweater, immaculate as usual. And beautiful. Always beautiful.

"Yes." It seemed the best answer at that moment. Eve's mouth was dry which made it difficult to speak. Finish it, that inner voice cried, now, Eve. Put an end to it.

"You're a courageous woman," Ruth said.

"Person," Eve answered. "I'm a courageous person. Why does it matter that I'm a woman?"

Ruth chuckled. "Sorry. Raw nerve?"

"Yes, very raw." Eve feigned a smile. "It's all right, I'm teasing you."

Eve saw Ruth glance round nervously. "If there are any press here tonight, I didn't send for them. The trouble is these things leak out."

"I know."

"What do you think this will achieve?"

"Not much," Eve said. "But it might change one person's mind, just one kid who sees what knives and guns really do, beyond killing someone, I mean."

"Yeah. Let's hope it does. Whatever it achieves, it will help Vicky." Ruth paused and regarded Eve carefully. "You seem a little down."

Eve shrugged. This was not the time and place to examine their relationship. "Tired."

"As long as that's all it is."

"It is." Eve quickly refocussed on the reason they were here. "I'm not so sure, about this."

"This?"

For a moment, Eve was given the chance she didn't want, but knew she should take. One word, that was all that was necessary. Us. All she had to say was us and it would be done.

Small word, huge consequences; heartbreak, loneliness, grief.

"Vicky, what she wants to do tonight," she said.

"Ah." Was that relief? "In what way are you unsure?"

"She's too in control. It worries me. A few days ago, she was angry and sobbing and completely broken. How she was the other day, when we both ended up at her flat…It didn't seem right."

"You know her better than I do."

Yes, Eve mused. I do.

"Look," Ruth said. "I know I've charged into this, or it seems that way. I was a bit impulsive and I'm worried that I could have caused some damage. I just hope I haven't encouraged Vicky to do something counter-productive."

"She's going to do it with or without us," Eve said. "I should stop worrying."

They found Vicky and about fifty people gathered by the entrance to Emerson. Most looked to be residents. They stood on the roadway at the edge of the triangle, quietly talking amongst themselves. Vicky's daughters were there. The rest were a mixture of the middle-aged, elderly and a scattering of those in their thirties. There were more women than men. The atmosphere was one of determination.

There were others standing slightly apart from the rest. Eve saw cameras, and microphones. They were obviously the press.

"I thought you said they weren't going to be here," Eve said.

Ruth looked worried. "I didn't call them."

"Vicky?" Eve said.

Ruth sighed. "Probably."

"Well, we're stuck with them now, so may as well put on a show. You should say something to them. I'll stay out of sight."

Eve felt Ruth's hand on her arm, briefly, lightly, but it was enough. Ruth then gathered herself together and strode over to the waiting journalists. They immediately closed in on her and began pummelling her with questions. Eve was surprised that this was such a story for them. But then again, it was late summer. News was like a drought-stricken waterhole this time of the year. Ruth called Vicky over and put her arm about her shoulders and presented her as the energy behind this event. For a moment, Eve was stricken with the thought that she might turn the press's attention on her as well, but the moment passed.

Or so she thought, because suddenly, she heard Vicky saying her name, loudly.

"Come over here, Reverend. I couldn't have done this without your support." She returned her attention to the cameras. "Reverend Eve is a hero. She should be honoured by the Queen for what she has done for this community. Come on, Eve. Don't be shy."

Eve had no choice. The crowd of Vicky's neighbours and supporters opened to let her through. She felt their pats on her back. Someone grabbed her hand and squeezed it. Then she found herself before a wall of cameras and microphones.

Vicky engulfed her in a hug. Eve felt the woman's genuine love and gratitude in the gesture and experienced a pang of guilt at being annoyed by the woman.

Questions were shouted at her and she managed to mumble embarrassingly modest answers about doing God's work. The journalists quickly lost interest and a moment later, Vicky and her entourage of press, neighbours and supporters were moving out into the triangular shared area of the flats.

"See them, out there?" Vicky proclaimed to the nearest microphone and indicated towards the centre of the triangle. "Every night it's the same."

There were cars on the grass, parked about the so-called sculpture. Most had their engines running. Music pulsed from one of them, loud, repetitive and bass-heavy. A voice rapped angrily over the rhythm. The group of youths stood around or sat on the grass or on the bonnets of the cars and waited.

"Best we stay at the back for now," Eve said.

Ruth nodded. She seemed nervous. "I'm not sure about this," she said.

"You scared?"

"No, it's not that. It's Vicky. Something's off-kilter."

The group reached the youths and cars in the middle of the triangle and stopped a few yards from them. The youths did nothing but stare and snigger to each other. The music went on, deafening. Bass thudded through the ground and up into Eve's gut.

"I'd like to talk to you," Vicky said. She spoke loudly enough to be heard above the din and with enough authority for the youths to drop their studied disinterest.

"Yeah? What about?" The speaker was a muscular-looking

male of about twenty. His head was shaved, and his skin was pale and unhealthy looking. He glared at Vicky and took a step towards her.

"I'm Nathan Steel's mother," she said.

A shrug. A smirk. Someone sniggered. Vicky didn't blink. She reached inside her coat and drew out a small urn. She held it up in front of her, high so all could see.

"This is my son," she said.

No. This was bad. Eve was torn. She should intervene. She should stop this. She saw Ruth move close to Vicky. She saw her try to speak to her.

Now the gang were interested. Eve heard a startled, "What's in there then?"

"My son was murdered for a few ounces of weed. For…" Vicky's voice was breaking. "He will never get married. He will never have children. Just because some evil little bastard decided that he should be killed. And you know who did it? Don't you."

She was aggressive now, confrontational.

The leader made calming motions with his hands. "Woah, wait a minute." His accent was thick with the strange fake West Indian patois beloved of the young. Eve had never heard such accent or phrasing from anyone with a genuine Caribbean heritage. "You blaming us?" He sounded genuinely outraged. Hurt, almost.

"You know who did it, and you won't tell the police. Because you're cowards."

There were angry shouts of support from the people behind her.

Eve sensed Ruth's tension. She forced her way through the

residents towards Vicky. The gang were all on their feet now. "You calling us cowards? That's disrespect, you old bitch."

"You don't deserve respect. Because you won't protect your own. Because you won't go to the police."

"We don't have no business with the feds –"

"Feds? Grow up!" Vicky shouted. Her anger was on the surface now. It was spreading out through her group. "They're the police. They don't want to –"

"Fuck off. Go on, piss off and leave us alone."

"This is my son!" Vicky almost screamed then wrenched off the lid of the urn and thrust it outwards towards the leader. Ash billowed out. She rushed forwards, shaking it at the youths. Who shouted in disgust and flinched away? The leader stumbled back, coughing. His face grey from the ash, which had covered him.

"You disgusting old bitch," he yelled and went for her. Someone stepped in, a middle-aged man, tall and broad. He collided with the leader and there was a scuffle. Others launched themselves into the mad swirling brawl. There was pushing and kicking, but no punching. This was a real fight, not some sanitised Hollywood punch-up. It was messy and clumsy accompanied by loud shouting and screaming.

Knives. Eve suddenly realised that the gang probably carried knives. She made to rush forward, shouting Vicky's name. Someone held her back. Ruth. She had a phone in one hand, clamped to her ear. Eve heard her shout the word police into it.

Someone else must have heard, because the youths suddenly broke away and fled towards the far corners of the triangle and into the gathering darkness. A couple of residents set off in pursuit, but soon gave up, mostly bent double hands on thighs, gasping for breath.

The press was moving in now. Cameras flashed. Questions were being shouted.

Eve held on to Ruth and hurried her away towards the shadows. A camera flashed in her face.

Chapter Seven: The Choice

Eve stood outside the front door of the cottage and stared at the sky. It was morning, cold but already bright. The sky was an unbroken blue dome that stretched over the endless landscape of ploughed fields. It was empty, not only of cloud but of aircraft contrails, of the distant sliver glint of airliners and of birds. This whole place was empty.

Yet it wasn't, was it? God was here. She smiled, warmed by the memory of last night. This was her future. She had tasted her own eternity and it had been bliss. She was impatient for it, but also uneasy.

As she stood there, Eve wondered if this place existed only in her mind. Was she in some coma-like state? Drugged? Hypnotised? She pulled her parka tighter about herself and tried to remember the invitation to come here. There was a memory. She had received an email from Angela.

"Dear Reverend Eve Clements. I am the Deacon at St Jude's, a small parish in deepest Suffolk. We have heard about your good works at St Martin's, and about your present difficulties, and would be honoured if you would take up the mantle for us here. We have a fully furnished rectory and a

loving and faithful congregation. I understand that this is a
very different parish to the one you are accustomed to but feel
you would fit in perfectly. Please give our invitation serious
consideration. Take your time but know that we are keen to
meet you. Yours in Christ, Angela Pullman"

"Your present difficulties"? How did she know about
those? Bishop Paul? Probably. A word with the deacon of
the most obscure, out-of-the-way parish in the country? A
place where he could be rid of that troublesome priest, Eve
Clements? That would, of course, work if this was a normal
out-of-the-way parish, but it wasn't.

Her vivid memory of the email, of her decision to take up
the offer without even visiting the parish, her desperate need
to get away from the field of pain, made it worse. It made this
place real.

And that sky? The heavenly battleground, the sighting of
her mother, the things trying to get into the cottage? Her mind
was troubled. She had suffered loss and stress. Hallucination.
It had to be. Perhaps, she should embrace it. Perhaps it was
something she needed to go through. There were stories of
religious men and women who had shut themselves off from
the world and experienced visions and fought titanic spiritual
battles. Christ had taken himself off into the wilderness for
more than a month and there battled the Devil. She had to see
this as her own wilderness.

Literal as well as figurative.

Eve shrugged and set off towards the church. She would
meditate in that place. She would pray and read and try to
absorb the feel of the building. It too was a strange place, but
it was a church.

Inside, it was peaceful. Eve walked slowly down the aisle and stopped before the simple altar and that strange stained-glass window. She focused her attention on the point where the woman's hands met the hand from the well. She saw how tightly they were grasped. There was something odd about the woman. Eve moved closer, frustrated that she could not see the portrait's face in the shadowed interior of the hood. She came to the altar and stared up and saw that there were fissures in the woman's robe and in her hand. Hairline cracks webbed over her skin. The wounds did not bleed but glimpsed through the openings was light. Reddish-orange. Fire.

The door slammed shut.

"You know who that is, don't you?"

She started, swung round to see Angela retracing her own steps along the aisle.

"Sorry," she said. I didn't mean to startle you."

"It's okay. I didn't hear you come in."

I didn't hear your car either, Eve told her silently.

"Just checking in," Angela said. "I won't stay long"

Eve was irritated now. She didn't need checking. She wasn't a child, but on the other hand, it was good to know that she wasn't completely alone out here. A fine hermit she would make. "What did you mean, that I should know who that woman is?"

Angela was standing beside her now.

"It's you."

This time Eve laughed. "Me? I wouldn't be seen dead wearing that colour." Facetiousness, her last weapon of defiance.

"You sound sceptical."

"I am. Unless you commissioned it just before I arrived, it's highly unlikely that the artist, or glazier or whatever the people who make these things are, would have heard of me."

"It's five hundred years old," Angela said. "But it is you."

"How do you know? You can't see her face, its hidden by the hood of her robe." She stared at it, uneasy again. "All right, I can understand that it is symbolic, the priest of the parish, helping rescue souls from Hell. That's what you said the first time we stood here. Is that what you mean?"

There was no answer. Angela was gone.

Eve scanned the church then ran back to the door and outside. There was no sign of Angela's car. There was no sign that she had even been here at all. Eve was not frightened now. She was angry. She wanted an answer and suddenly she knew how to get it.

Of course, the bishop wanted to see her.

He was surprisingly calm when she was shown into his cosy study. There was a coffee waiting for her. Black, no sugar, just as she liked it. He said nothing but waited while she drank a little then sat down himself. This time at his chair on the far side of his desk.

"You know why I want to talk to you, don't you?" He wounded regretful rather than angry.

"Yes. The Vicky Steel disaster." At least, she hoped that was what it was.

"What were you thinking, Eve?"

"I wanted to support her. I thought she was going to talk to the gang. I thought she was going to reach out to them in some way."

"You must have known."

"How?" Too sharp, too defensive. Eve swallowed and forced herself to let Bishop Paul have the next word.

"You're not a fool…Well, not usually. Surely there must have been a sign that she was planning something like this."

"She seemed genuine. I can't read minds, Bishop."

"You can read people's faces well enough. You can hear what they are really saying That's why you've been so successful in your parish. You know, you feel."

This was the closest Paul had ever come to offering her praise and Eve felt unsettled by it.

He sighed and picked up the newspaper that lay on his desk. "And this picture, how do you explain this? A member of the clergy, arm in arm with a politician? A potential MP?"

"I can't help it if an MP decides to turn up."

A moment. The air seemed to stretch tight. Eve held Paul's long, hard stare.

"There are those who want you out. Or put somewhere where you can do no harm."

"Like Van Gogh, is that it?"

"Van Gogh?"

"He was a Lutheran minister long before he was an artist. His church didn't like the fact that he lived as the poorest of his parishioners did. They thought it was undignified and they threw him out."

"This is different."

"How?"

Eve was hurt, but she was damned if she was going to let him see it.

"Who cares about one vicar in one parish in London, a

parish no one cares about anyway?"

"You're bringing the church into disrepute –"

"Good."

"What?"

"I'm glad I'm bringing the church into disrepute. It needs to be in disrepute. It needs to fight, not kow-tow."

"Eve," Paul said, his voice low and ominous. "Go back to your parish. This is your last chance. No more controversy. Do your good works but do them quietly. Do you understand?"

Eve stood and made for the door.

"And stay away from that woman."

She was suddenly afraid. She was under scrutiny. It was inevitable that her affair with Ruth Chandler would be found out and then that would be the end.

When she arrived home and shut the door to her flat, she felt safe. There was a measure of peace in here. But not for long, she knew. Eve crossed to the small space between her sofa and desk. She dropped to her knees and closed her eyes and stayed that way without speaking or moving until her breathing steadied and her mind cleared.

She prayed. She begged God to listen and to give her wisdom and the strength she would need once she received that wisdom. She pleaded with the darkness. She confessed her sin, she begged forgiveness. She promised to repent. She could not be taken from her calling. Her life was formed of this.

Eve prayed all night. She fell asleep on her knees and woke sometime in those small dark hours she had loved as a child. She drank cola and made a jam sandwich for old times' sake then prayed again.

God gave no indication that he heard her, but that was faith wasn't it?

"Hi honey, I'm home," Ruth called out in her usual mock-American accent as she entered the flat, two nights later. Doors opened and closed. "God, that was an ordeal." She had been to a Labour Party function. Part of the job.

Eve listened to Ruth's approach from the minute box-room she used as her office. It was almost midnight. Eve was at her desk, as usual, although this evening her computer screen was ignored, her sermon notes unheeded. She had achieved nothing but had no idea where else to be while she waited for Ruth to arrive.

"Hi," Eve called back. She was surprised at how she managed to keep her voice steady.

"Coffee?"

"No, thanks. I…Ruth. I need to talk to you."

A moment, then Ruth's footsteps sounded along the stunted passageway between the kitchen and the office.

The door opened. Eve didn't want to look at her but forced herself to turn and watch as Ruth came in. She looked lovely. She wore her black faux fur and a maroon dress. She had wanted to take Eve with her, but that would not have been wise.

"What's wrong?" Ruth said. "You don't look well."

Eve took a deep, steadying breath. Was she going to say this? Yes, of course she was. She wanted to cry but held her emotions tight to herself.

"I have to choose, Ruth. You or the church."

Please make this easy. Please…

"So, he's forced you to leave the church, after all you've achieved –"

"No, Ruth, you don't understand."

"Yes, I do. The Bishop is a homophobic moron and wants you to give up your job because he doesn't like you dating a woman."

"He doesn't know about you and…This is my calling. I can't turn my back on it. I'm sorry. I…"

Ruth paled. "No, Eve, you're not listening –"

"Ruth, you're the one who isn't listening." She had been, of course. She knew exactly what Eve was telling her. It was just that it was too terrible for her to acknowledge.

"You're leaving me?" Ruth said quietly. "You're choosing… You're choosing a fairy tale over reality?"

"Please, Ruth. I'm sorry. I don't know what to do. But this is me. This church. My faith…"

"Oh, don't be sorry. Don't pretend you're torn between me and your fucking God."

The anger was breaking through. Eve got to her feet. She was crying now. She wanted Ruth to stay. She couldn't be alone anymore. But she could never turn her back on God, on her calling, on the people who needed her and relied on her.

Ruth pushed her away, not hard, but enough for Eve to get the message; no kiss, no last hug.

"I'll leave you to it then," Ruth said brusquely. "And carry on down the road to Hell. Enjoy your holiness." Ruth spun about and stepped out into the passage. In a moment, she was out of the flat and on the landing. "Enjoy Heaven, Saint-fucking-Eve." Her voice echoed against the stairway's concrete walls. "I was going to leave him for you."

Eve followed her. "Ruth. Ruth. Ruth."

Ruth clattered down the stairs, her coat billowed. In a moment, she was gone.

She was gone.

Dear God, gone.

She hadn't looked back. That hurt more than any of this. She had not even glanced over her shoulder, as she fled Eve's presence. She had taken nothing, none of the clothes or other possessions she had left here. She would have to come back to do that. She would have to return to the flat and retrieve the parts of it that were her. She would need to strip the place of every trace of herself.

A howl of utter, formless despair tore itself from Eve's throat and drove her to her knees on the landing. She howled and cursed God and sobbed until there was nothing left. Then she prayed and no one listened

Drank

Hauled herself into her pulpit and preached.

Threw herself into her work.

Prayed and begged and pleaded.

Drank.

Worked.

Drank.

Drank.

Preached.

Prayed.

Drank.

Then, one Sunday morning, she collapsed in the pulpit and it was over.

Chapter Eight: The Village

Eve walked.

Once again, she followed the lane that led away from the church to God knew where.

But do You know? she asked Him silently. Or are you as confused as I am? Is that why you didn't come near me after Ruth walked out? Is that why my prayers were cries of pain that bounced off the ceiling and rained back down on me? Because You didn't know how to help.

Or didn't *want* to help?

There was a wager to win, wasn't there? Your little bet with Satan that I couldn't be broken. Well, don't worry about it. You won. I never stopped praying. I never stopped believing. Even when I was so drunk, I pissed the bed and even when I was so hungover and grief stricken, I couldn't get out of the bloody bed at all. I still cried out to you. I still begged you for help. Begged and pleaded. I still washed my face and climbed into that pulpit every Sunday and managed to mumble something that resembled a sermon, until Bishop Paul was able to rid himself of that troublesome priest by suspending me on health grounds. For my own good, he said, so that I could seek help and reflect on my future. And still I prayed and tried to trust you and reached out for you because there was nothing else.

After some immeasurable passage of time, Eve felt that same change in the air as she had experienced last time. The same chill breeze. The same taste of imminent rain.

She zipped up her parka and a few minutes later, drew the hood up over her head. The cold burrowed deep through the quilted material, through the wool and cotton she wore and into her flesh.

The first drop of rain stung Eve's face. The wind strengthened. The leading edge of light grey cloud appeared in the strip of sky visible between the tall hedgerows. A warning? She should not be doing this. She had been given a chance. She had been brought closer to God than she could ever have imagined possible this side of the grave and here she was being utterly disobedient.

Her legs ached. She shivered and flinched against the bullets of rain the wind drove into her face. It pattered on the hood of her coat. It beat at her legs. The cloud darkened. The wind strengthened.

This was hopeless. Any moment now she would turn a corner and find herself back at the church –

Not this time. "Mum." Her cry was far from plaintive. It was a demand. She was tired and angry. "Mum. *Mum*."

Nothing.

So, did these hallucinations, these visits from the Great Beyond, only happen when they wanted them to? The ubiquitous, spiritual *they*. To hell with them. Eve walked faster, head down, hands rammed deep into her coat pockets. The wind pummelled her like a boxer. The rain scoured her face through the fur-edged oval through which she saw the world.

Then she smelled cheap perfume. Then she *felt* her.

Mum. There, in the road ahead. Gaunt, pale and ill. Right arm with its cigarette hand cradled in her left hand. Hair blown wild by the storm. Trakkie on. She smiled at her daughter then turned and strode on ahead into the rain and wind. Her movements were effortless while Eve was bent before the gale.

Mum swung suddenly to the left, appeared to step into the tangle of leafless thorn that was the hedge and was gone. Eve broke into a run, soon breathless because it seemed as though the faster she ran, the stronger the gale became. She drove herself on until she felt as if she had almost reached an impasse, her own effort and the force of the wind equalised.

She staggered to the point at which Mum had disappeared and saw a break in the hedge. It revealed a lane that rose steeply and was even narrower than the one she had walked so far. Mum was there, waiting. The same distance ahead of her. Eve stepped into the lane. Mum resumed walking. The slope was steeper than it looked and, already out of breath from fighting the gale, Eve felt as if the last of her strength was draining away. The rain lashed at her face. It was difficult to see now. Her feet were soaked. Water ran down the hill in wavelets. The hedges on either side strained and hissed. The light was dim and dusk-like. Mum seemed unaffected, however. She strode on, not looking back. Eve struggled in her wake. The lane became narrower and narrower. Branches plucked at her coat. Exhausted, she felt her legs give way. She almost fell but swore at herself to keep going. Foul words,

but she needed anger now. Surely God wasn't such a delicate
flower that a few expletives would hurt Him

Then it ended.

Eve stumbled out into a wider, more open road and was
momentarily confused by a roar and the blare of a horn. She
jumped back as a lorry thundered past. The horn blared again,
a last shout of annoyance at her stupidity.

Eve stared after it. This was the first vehicle she had seen
since she had stepped off that train at Weddon Station, other
than Angela's car and the sound of the bible group visitors
arriving and leaving the other night. She realised then that she
hadn't actually seen their cars and for a moment was troubled
by the idea that they had not driven to the rectory but had
somehow appeared out of nowhere and faked the gravel-
crunching and door slamming for her benefit.

Recovered from her near-miss, Eve and stood at the
junction and tried to grasp what she saw. The road stretched
left and right. There were no houses in sight. There were fields
and, directly opposite, a wood. There were sounds, distant
cars, one approaching. There were birds. Rooks by the look
and sound of them, wheeling about the denuded treetops,
black and angular against the grey sky.

The storm had ceased. There was a breeze and it was cold,
but there was no gale here. No rain.

Mum was nowhere in sight. Eve had last seen her standing
on the far side of the road at the entrance to a wooded path.
Presumably she was meant to cross. Eve looked left and right.
She saw a car in the distance but there was plenty of time. It
felt strangely comforting to gently race an oncoming vehicle.
Come to that, apart from the lorry that had almost killed her,

when was the last time she had shared a road with a vehicle of any kind?

Eve reached the far side well ahead of the car. She waited for it to pass, an odd need to reassure herself that it was real, that it had a driver who was someone other than the handful of people she had met since she arrived. Five seconds, six, then it was close enough for her to see that it contained a family. It was driven by a woman, presumably the mother, who sat beside a tall, balding man who wore sunglasses, even though the sun could hardly be described as dazzling at the moment.

The car hissed by. Eve glimpsed children. She watched it race into the distance and disappear.

Silence again. No, this silence wasn't complete. This silence didn't cloy and suffocate. This was riddled with sound, the hiss and creak of branches in the breeze, the distant drone of cars and lorries, the slow scratch of an aircraft, a dog's bark. Eager to encounter other human beings, Eve set off into the wood.

After a few moments she heard a crunching sound. She turned to see two cyclists, each clad in their official uniform of lycra, neon-rimmed, reflective goggles, and helmet (complete with camera). They waved a greeting as they rode past her. People. *Other* people. Eve felt like a survivor from some mountain plane crash who had found civilisation at last.

The wind strengthened, changing the trees' graceful wave to agitation. Even so, Eve felt no threat in the breeze. She walked on, tired, wet and cold, but reassured, until she emerged from the wood and found herself on a broad open grassy strip. To her right there were more trees and glimpsed between them, brown ploughed fields.

To her left, there was a high grassy bank that extended as far as she could see. Something caught her eye and she saw Mum again, standing on the summit of the bank. There were steps cut into the grass. Eve climbed. It was somewhere between ten and twenty feet. Hard to tell, and she wasn't counting.

When she came to the top, she saw a vast expanse of water. The far bank was greyed by distance. Wind ruffled the surface. There were a handful of dinghies out there. She heard the dog bark again. She saw other walkers. None of them close.

Mum stood next to a sign. Eve walked up to it. Startled by the way she had come to accept the *dead* woman's presence, a dead woman. Ghost or hallucination, Mum seemed real at that moment. The wind plucked at her hair. However, as she came closer, Eve saw that the borders of Mum's body were unstable. They bled matter into the grey air like smoke. There was sadness on Mum's face. And strain, as if she struggled to hold onto this form but was losing her battle.

Eve reached out towards the woman, deceit, whatever she or it was, and felt Mum's fingers meet her own. They clasped hands. Eve felt the substance of the other woman drain through her grip and there was a moment, an instant when she felt Mum pass over and through her. A moment of intense sensation and familiarity.

Then she was gone.

Eve stood stock still for a moment, waiting until she could regain control. It was hard. She didn't want control. She wanted tears and weakness. She wanted collapse and oblivion.

She wanted Mum.

Breathing hard, reluctant, afraid, Eve turned to look at the map and information board.

Weddon Waters. Constructed in 1973 and named after the village which was demolished to make way for the reservoir. No trace remains of Weddon or its two churches; the more recent, St Michael's, which was completed in 1858, and the older St Jude's, which was located approximately 1.5 miles from the village centre. St Jude's was de-sanctified in the 18th Century, after claims that it was haunted and had become the meeting place for a witches' coven. The church and its adjacent rectory were allowed to fall into ruin. These ruins were left intact during the reservoir construction to save on costs. This has given rise to local stories of ghostly church bells and choir song coming from the waters on each anniversary of the flooding of Weddon.

Chapter Nine: Things Will Be Broken

The storm broke with little warning. A gust of wind and a sudden darkening of the sky. The surface of the reservoir grew rough and broken by waves. The dinghies bobbed and yawed perilously and hurried for shore. People ran, huddled into their coats. The dog's bark became fearful. Then the rain came. It was like an explosion, a torrent poured out of the clouds as if emptied from some great lake in the sky beyond.

Eve turned and stumbled towards the woods. She was confused, shocked and unable to think clearly. There was no reality anymore. Her parish lay under the restless grey waters of that reservoir and her church was, at best, a submerged ruin.

She reached the woods and fell against the nearest of the trees. Its groans and creaks were cries of pain, heard and felt through the rough bark of its immense trunk. Thunder exploded across the indigo sky. There was no shelter here. You weren't supposed to hide under trees in electrical storms, were you?

A flash of lightning. Bright enough to draw Eve's gaze. The light tore a hole into the sky and through it, Eve saw figures, immense, glowing, terrible and beautiful. The light was momentary, yet in that instant, Eve once again saw a battle. A struggle between titanic creatures whose geometries were vast and incomprehensible.

They were aware of her. They had ceased their fight and turned to look down on her.

She plunged into the woods, slashed by branches, stumbling over fallen logs and grabbed-at by tentacles of dead, brown bracken. She could feel them coming, striding through the clouds, bearing down on her.

She all but fell out of the woods and onto the road. The entrance to the pathway was nowhere in sight. There was nothing but the icy deluge, the rage of the gale, the boiling, thunderous cloud and the lightning that gave sight of her monstrous pursuers

A horn blared. There was a wash of headlights. She looked back to see a car, low-slung and loud race out of the murk. It squealed to a halt a few feet away. A door opened. A figure leaned out and called her name.

Angela.

Eve fled. She would follow the road. Wave down the next vehicle she saw. The rain was now a relentless waterfall that seemed to tear open her clothes and flesh with arctic ferocity. The gale was a solid wall against which she strained and staggered. The lightning sizzled and burned the air and danced electricity on her flesh. She tried not to look up, but the compulsion was too strong.

The beauty of the creatures made her weep. Their awful power reduced her to a fear so primal, it felt like madness.

She wasn't aware of her collapse. Suddenly she was

face down in the rushing, cold stream of rainwater, grazed and bruised against the hard tarmac beneath. A great light unfolded around her. She lay motionless as it seeped into her body and warmed every part of her. She wanted to let go and surrender to whatever glory had come for her. All the pain and heartache she had endured since that terrible morning when the Shouting People had burst in and ripped her life apart, all the sorrow at her sacrifice and loss, dissolved and her tears were wiped away.

Not yet.

She felt a hand on her shoulder then she was in Angela's arms and being carried towards the storm-blurred headlights of the woman's car.

But soon.

She sat, hunched in the passenger seat, and shivered. The heating was on. The car raced along the lanes. Angela said nothing. The light outside was dull and the scenery blurred by the storm.

The church appeared. St Jude's, the church that should not exist. Angela swung the car skilfully into the driveway and crunched to a halt close to the front door of the vicarage.

"Were they rebuilt?" It was the first time Eve had spoken. Her voice was dulled by exhaustion.

"*Here*, they were never a ruin."

Rain hammered at the car roof. The scene outside was washed into a blur by the waves of water that streamed over the windscreen.

"Here?"

"We need to get you indoors. You're soaked through and

you're freezing, Eve. You'll be ill –"

"What is *here*?"

A moment. A resigned sigh.

"It's a Place that lies between the shadows and angles of the world. It's where the reality you know feeds. Where its roots lie. What happens here is intimately tied to what happens on the surface."

Eve was tired of hints and innuendo, and of loss, guilt and grief. She wanted the light. She wanted to return to its embrace.

"Not yet. I'm sorry, Eve."

So, Angela really could read her mind.

"We need you here."

"What for?"

"The congregation here, they are…lost souls in need of redemption."

"The Bible has the answer. Believe in Jesus –"

"– and you will be saved." Angela held Eve's hand. Her grip was firm and despite herself, Eve found comfort in the contact. "True for most people," Angela continued. "But not for your congregation."

The storm had eased to a chill breeze. The clouds were blown into ragged strips and blue sky was revealed.

"Your congregation, the people you met the other night, they are…their need is *particular*. The usual route to salvation doesn't apply to them."

"How can I help them?"

"You've remained faithful despite your trials and suffering. That makes you a channel, a vessel through which God can reach down and save these people from Hell. They want to throw in their lot with Him. But they need a special redemption. That is, you."

"They can't be in Hell? I saw them the other night…" Eve stopped speaking because she had run out of words.

"They showed themselves in a way you could understand, but what you saw were shadows. Those people, the forms they took, are as far they can reach into this world."

"Who are they, Angela?"

"You wouldn't under –"

"No more bloody mysteries. Tell me who they are."

A moment. Then; "Fallen angels."

"What? You mean, those people… those people are…" She remembered the old lady, the glimpse. the sudden sense that more lay beyond the borders of her-self than frail, aging flesh.

Angels?

"Are you an…"

Angela smiled and then shrugged. "You know, of course, all about the war in Heaven."

"Lucifer became filled with pride and thought himself as powerful as God. He was cast out."

"Yes, yes he was. He fell to Earth, which is how the Bible interprets something that is beyond human comprehension. The nearest thing I can give you to understanding the scale of this is to read universe for earth. It wasn't golden-haired, winged beauties wrestling with horned little creatures armed with pitchforks. When those angels fell, holes were punched in the fabric. It was cataclysmic, apocalyptic. The war didn't end there. It has raged ever since, on an epic scale and right here, in the hearts and souls of the creation. But the victory can be won. In Hell, whatever you want to call it, the lower strata of the under-verse, whatever helps you understand, there are angels who want to change sides, who are tired of the struggle, and who want to return to their creator. A bridge is needed."

"A bridge? Me?" The single syllable reeked of vanity and idiocy in equal measure, to Eve. Her? A bridge between Heaven and Hell? *Her?* Human. Flawed, flesh and bone, ordinary, tiny, angry *her?*

"Yes. You, Eve. There's a certain irony in that name. Perhaps the seed was put into your mother's mind by the Spirit. I'm not party to such things."

"But how do I do this?"

"When the moment comes, you will know. You will extend your hand, draw these souls from the Pit and free them to walk the earth. The stalemate, the balance will be broken."

Eve tried to hold onto the concept. The attempt was futile. Instead she asked a question that seemed utterly selfish but needed to be asked. She was also afraid of the answer.

"When…When this is done, what happens to me?"

"You?" Angela's arm was about her shoulders, pulling her close. "You will be transformed, transfigured. You will know the ecstasy of the divine. You have no home, not on Earth, Eve, not anymore. You will know bliss. I promise. The pain will be over."

"That's what people say to the dying."

"You're are not going to die. You will be filled with the spirit, you will be safe, and you will be translated, like Elijah, and Enoch."

Eve closed her eyes and pondered this. The final aim of

her spiritual life, Heaven. The presence of God, translation into a spiritual being and without the pain and darkness of dying.

"And…and if I can't do this?"

A pause. Another of Angela's shrugs. "Then you'll remain on Earth. Flesh. Waiting for death and fighting the battle for decades to come. Seeking redemption. Waiting on God's pleasure as to whether he accepts you or not." Angela turned, more earnest now. "The war is growing intense. There will be shockwaves, it will affect your world. If you believe it to be dark now…You have no conception of what it will become."

"I don't know…" Eve said. "Angela, I don't…"

Angela didn't answer. Eve got out of the car and knew long before she turned round to close its door that the vehicle and its driver were gone.

*

The flint wall of St Jude's was rough under Eve's hands. Rough and oh, so solid. She pressed harder. The wall's solidity remained. Surely it should melt away like the stone-fleshed ghost it was. The church was not real. Yet here, now, under the pale cloudless dome of winter sky, the church existed.

Afraid, Eve headed back towards the cottage. As she walked, she looked across the fields. As always, those ploughed brown oceans were still and silent, and infinite, or so it seemed. Perhaps they were, in this Place, as Angela had called it. There was no telling how time and space worked here.

There was no trace of the storm, other than the puddles and general wetness of the ground. The air was fresh, knife-

edged, reviving, and pure. She stood with her back to the
cottage door and breathed deep. Prison, parallel universe
whatever this place was, it was certainly not a Bad Place.
Alarming, frightening at times, but no one here sought her
harm. The storms were the guard dogs, perhaps. Making sure
she didn't stray. Well, they had almost lost her this morning.

Cold now, Eve turned and went indoors. She headed
into the sitting room and set about lighting a fire; crumpled
paper, kindling stacked into a rough wigwam, match applied
to the paper. She felt absurdly pleased when it caught. In a
few seconds, the wood began to snap and crack. Cautiously,
she added larger pieces of wood. She went into the kitchen
to make coffee then, when she returned, added coal. The
flames disappeared, replaced by curls of grey-white smoke.
She sighed, annoyed with herself for having ruined her good
work. But then the first flame broke through. Success. A small
victory. Something under her control.

The absurdity hit her then. Here she was in some parallel
universe, pleased with herself for lighting a fire.

Small steps. Normality.

She went upstairs to shower and change her clothes. Then
went back, made coffee, and set up her notes and sermon-
making equipment on the coffee table in the sitting room. She
did not pray. She couldn't, not yet. She would write a sermon.
It would probably never be preached but it would channel her
thoughts.

She picked up her bible. She needed something to comfort
her, a passage from the New Testament. Words spoken by
Jesus.

It fell open on Job Chapter One. Annoyed, she closed it

again and retried, this time making sure she prised it apart
deep into where she knew the Gospels to be.

Job Chapter One.

A waft of cheap perfume.

A third attempt, this time at the very beginning, Genesis.

Job Chapter One.

The perfume smell grew stronger.

Mum, no. Leave me alone now. Please.

The storm erupted suddenly outside. It was early, there was
still light out there, grey and faltering, but daylight, nonetheless.
The tempest battered at the windows and thudded against the
walls as if angry and desperate to get in. Eve fought down her
panic. What was she going to do, run outside? Throw herself
once more into the freezing rain and hurricane grade winds.

Job Chapter One.

She began to read that odd, inconsistent opening.

*There was a man in the land of Uz, whose name was Job; and that
man was perfect and upright, and one that feared God, and eschewed evil.*

She was meant to read this chapter. Yet, it didn't feel right.
It didn't feel wholesome. The strength and rage of the storm
sounded like anger. Eve was being shown something. But not
by Heaven.

Which was nonsense, of course.

*Now there was a day when the sons of God came to present themselves
before the Lord, and Satan came also among them.*

The sons of God? Names given to the fallen angels in
Genesis. Those sons? And Satan, in the presence of God?
This was where it all went wrong, or strange. A meeting of
the two sides. Sworn enemies, light and dark, good and evil,
in the same room, in talks. Peace talks perhaps, like the South

and North Vietnamese in Paris? Talks that eventually come around to one individual.

And the Lord said unto Satan, Whence comest thou? Then Satan answered the Lord, and said, From going to and fro in the earth, and from walking up and down in it.

Then God said to him; Hast thou considered my servant Job, that there is none like him in the earth, a perfect and an upright man, one that feareth God, and escheweth evil?

Then Satan answered the Lord, and said, Doth Job fear God for nought? Hast not thou made an hedge about him, and about his house, and about all that he hath on every side? Thou hast blessed the work of his hands, and his substance is increased in the land. But put forth thine hand now, and touch all that he hath, and he will curse thee to thy face.

And the Lord said unto Satan, Behold, all that he hath is in thy power; only upon himself put not forth thine hand. So Satan went forth from the presence of the Lord.

It was not an easy book. Job ended up sitting in a pile of ashes, complaining about his lot. But then, why shouldn't he? Surely, he was a pawn, ruthlessly thrown to the wolves simply to prove a point. And the ending, when his wealth and riches were returned, his reward for spirituality was a carnal one.

But wasn't this *her* story? The depths to which she had fallen after sending Ruth away. She could imagine Satan, a sort of otherworldly barrister, thumbs hooked in the front of his robe, striding back and forth before the Great Judge, making his case that the Reverend Eve Clements needed to have the mettle of her faith truly tested to ascertain its authenticity.

Well, she *had* held on. She had prayed even when it felt as if she was crying out into empty space. Now she had her reward. Direct access to the God who had been hidden behind the wall of faith until now.

Or was she simply a pawn in their divine game? Surely that was Job's role. A point of honour to be proved. A bet.

The madness of this place, and her fear of it, had diminished for now, replaced by anger. How dare they do this to her? Then the panic, never far from the surface, threatened to break through once more and Eve forced herself to calm down. There was nothing she could do about any of this. Certainly, there was no easy way out of here. The train station was under the water in that giant reservoir, along with the rest of the village it served. She could never make it back there. Even if she could fight her way through the inevitable storm, she had no idea where the exit to the real world was nor the strength to find it again. She had nowhere else to go but this cottage and church.

She had to trust God.

She had to trust Angela.

Eve closed the Bible and placed it back on the table. She half-expected to see it blown open by some freak gust of icy wind, pages rifled until it was, once again, offering her the story of the righteous man from Uz. She waited. Her Bible remained shut.

Outside, the light failed, and the storm gathered strength.

She stared into the fire, at the red-glowing landscapes that lay in the gaps between the coals and burning logs. She wondered if this was such a place, a non-world hidden in the gaps and folds of her own.

A loud snap woke her. Eve started, disorientated and aching. She blinked and became aware that she was still the armchair. The fire was reduced to a red glow, hot embers and the charred bulk of a log. Eve rubbed her eyes and tried to wake enough to get upstairs to bed. There would be no praying tonight. Sleep was what she needed.

The perfume smell strengthened.

She sat still. She listened for any clue that Mum was in the cottage. Nothing. Except the storm outside. She was so used to it now that she had to focus to hear it. There was someone in the cottage. She had no doubt about that. She could feel it and the feeling was strong.

Nothing for it. Eve got out of the chair and moved through the cottage to the kitchen. She stood at the door and reached for the switch. The light came on. Nothing. No sign of Mum. Upstairs then. She steeled herself then set off. Why was she so afraid? She had followed Mum earlier that day. She had come to her. Stood close to her.

This was different. She was indoors now, closed in. Trapped in here with a force that wanted to thwart her purpose. She reached the landing and paused. The perfume was stronger up here. She stood on the landing. Heart beating hard and fast. The bathroom and bedroom doors were all closed.

"Mum? Mum, are you there?"

There was no answer. But there was a sense that Mum had heard her and was waiting.

Eve crossed to the bedroom door, grabbed the latch and opened it.

Light on.

The bedroom was empty.

But it wasn't. She was here. No doubt of it. Her perfume was strong and sickly sweet, underlain now with the tang of weed. Her presence was intense. Eve spoke her name again.

And there was an answer, not audible, not speech, yet clear. There was no longer any sense of threat, yet she knelt and trembled, closed her eyes and whispered God's name.

This was a trial. A battle.

Something moved through the blackness. It was insubstantial. It was wreathed in familiar scents. It brought whispers and comforts. It brought Mum to her. There was no weight, yet she felt Mum's hand ruffle her hair, she felt her lips on her forehead. Mum held her close.

Don't upset the balance, sweetheart. It's been like that for a long, long time and it's how it all works. If you upset it, you'll break things.

She pushed at the thing that masqueraded as her mother and drove herself into the dark towards the light.

"Oh God, please help me."

"What's wrong?" Mum sounded hurt.

How could she do that? How could she hurt the woman she loved so much? Eve felt guilty.

Not real. *Not real.*

Deceit.

Lie.

"Leave me alone."

"Eve, please, don't make me cry…"

"*You are not Mum.*"

She was close, her face only inches from Eve's. She wanted to grab her and hold onto her. She wanted to draw her tightly to herself, but she didn't. She hauled herself towards the boiling light, towards the voices and warmth. She felt Mum's hand on her face. She closed her eyes and flinched back. Mum screamed. She howled and shrieked as she was dragged away. Even as Eve plunged into the heart of God, she saw the terrible desolation on Mum's face as she was hauled away, her heart torn to pieces by the realisation that she was losing her daughter.

Then Eve's tears were wiped away and the light and peace closed in about her and it was home.

*

Exhausted as she was from the battle, Eve couldn't sleep in her bed and dragged the duvet downstairs. She built up the fire, which was all but reduced to embers, then settled onto her knees. There was only one place of comfort and safety left to her now. Outside, the aeons-old war between Heaven and Hell raged on. The house shook, but Eve knew it wouldn't fall.

She laughed. She wanted to cry but she couldn't. She wanted Mum back but knew that would never, ever happen. She wanted Ruth, but that was over and could never be regained. She wanted to be far from here. She wanted to be done with her life, her flesh, her existence.

She was so lost.

She didn't have to be.

Perhaps this was the time. Now.

Swallowing dryly, weak from fear, Eve fought to still her mind. She felt the heat of the newly revived fire on the side of her face. She smelled the ashy, smoky smell of burning coal and smouldering wood.

The walls vibrated under the force of a powerful blow. She opened her eyes and turned to see the wall to the left of the fireplace bulge inwards then snap back as it was made of rubber. She realised that this reality, this place was beginning to crumble. Another blow. The thunder rumbled and lightning flickered and glowed for too long as if an atom bomb had exploded outside.

She closed her eyes and returned to the dark.

The cacophony outside began to fade. The light into which she plunged grew brighter. Voices, beautiful in their everlasting song, spiralled out of the glare. The volume grew until it was almost beyond endurance. The light burned her eyes through her tight closed lids. Something vast and terrible unfurled from the heart of the light. She wept and laughed as the blossoming form took shape. It was titanic in scale, something that had its borders in far galaxies, a swirling roaring explosion of energies. A boiling flower of flame. Its voice was the supernova explosion of stars. And its crushing regard was narrowed on her. On Eve.

Are you ready? Are you open and laid bare?

Yes, she cried-screamed-wept-whispered back. A form bust out of the flames, wings flapping. A beautiful, delicate being. A butterfly, fragile, aglow. It was gold, it shimmered and fluttered. Eve reached out to it. She saw her hand but knew that her hands were clasped together before her. She saw the being land on her upturned palm. She felt the tickle of its delicate, fibrous legs. She saw a final flutter of its wings and then it melted, suddenly, shockingly, into a pool of liquid gold, which burned its way into her flesh and was gone.

Not gone.

It surged through her veins. It lit up her nerves and shone bright in her mind. She opened her eyes and saw that her arms were outstretched, crucifix-style and she felt her fingers, strum the cords and thread that held together the universe.

Now. It was time.

Now.

*

"Then let's go," Angela said.

Angela?

Some distant part, some fleshy, earthbound part, of Eve was startled. She had no memory of the woman entering the cottage. Eve opened her eyes and looked up from where she knelt and Angela was there, as human and as ordinary as Angela could ever be in her expensive black coat and designer jeans. Her hand was extended. Eve accepted it and allowed Angela to help her to her feet.

All this seemed distant and remote from her, yet she felt the contact between them intensely. Her head was filled with song, a haunting, aching melody. The song was a cry, riven from a multitude of lips, a cry of joy and of unspeakable sadness. There was power in that song, too. It held the gift she had been given. It was the key that would unlock the gates of Hell and release penitent fallen angels. Eve curled herself about the song, protecting it within her core, as if it was a candle to be shielded from the breeze.

Still holding her hand, Angela led Eve through the cottage to the front door. Eve experienced a pang of sadness. As strange was this place was, it had become her home. She would never see it, or the world beyond, again. But what was out there for her? The people she loved had been taken. The church she had given her soul for was closed to her. No, this was the right way for her. The path she should tread. This was the culmination of her work.

"Hell won't let go of its own, easily," Angela spoke quietly, yet Eve heard every word with cut-crystal clarity. "Don't be frightened by what's out there. Don't be distracted or diverted. I'm with you. Okay? I'm by your side."

Eve daren't reply. To talk risked loosening her hold on the song. She felt Angela squeeze her hand.

The she wrenched the door open and they stepped outside.

Into a cataclysmic horror of noise and light.

There was no sense of time, only the darkness and gale-force winds and vicious, slashing rain. Lightning splintered the landscape and revealed glimpses of giant things advancing across the fields.

And, above, within the glare-riven clouds strode titanic beings that glowed golden with their own inner-light and whose dimensions and form were too vast and complex to comprehend in a moment.

Doubled over by the storm, wet and shivering but still consumed by the song, Eve stumbled in Angela's wake towards the church. Light, flooded from its windows, painted blue, red and green by the stained glass.

More light boiled and glowed over the fields to her left now. Streamers of it curled upwards towards the writhing clouds and stained their bellies with blood. There were cries of rage and pain. More fountains of scarlet light arced upwards from the ground and were answered by forks of jagged lightning from the glorious monsters in the clouds. Eve felt the shockwave from each clash as it blasted outwards and across the universe. The storm became even wilder.

Battered and struggling to breathe against the head-on, icy gale, Eve forced her concentration back on the church and on her mission. Nothing must distract her. The song filled her.

They reached the church and stepped inside.

The door slammed shut behind them.

Eve's congregation were already here. She didn't remember seeing their cars outside but wasn't surprised by that. They were the same disparate collection of characters that had met at her cottage two evenings ago. Harmless, nice people. They sat it the first three pews. and turned to watch her, expectantly.

Except they weren't harmless, nice people. The characters she saw sitting here, the elderly lady, the shy young man and woman, the successful couple, all these were masks.

They show themselves in a way you could understand, but what you see are shadows. Those people, the forms they take, are as far they can reach into this world.

They are a deceit.

The word cut through the song.

Deceit. Isn't that what Angela had called Mum? A deceit and a lie.

No, these were Fallen Angels. These were the penitent who wanted to return to their God and maker. The balance would be shifted, the forces of Satan outnumbered. Eve took her place before them. They gazed on her. They adored her. She felt the song rise in intensity.

She closed her eyes and felt the sacred words rise inside her. She spread her arms wide. And threw back her head and laughed from the sheer joy of it. And saw –

Mum, struggling and shrieking her name as she was dragged outside. Mum who loved her in her flawed, desperate, tender way.

Then she saw…

Leanne. There, hunched over, blood dripping from her broken nose. She trembled and hugged herself. She dragged her head up so that she could look directly into Eve's eyes and she said: "Help me."

The joy and the energy that coursed through her burned in her hands. She felt the very air around her stretch and tear. She saw the angels lurch to their feet, faces contorted into bliss. She heard and saw the great war outside. She felt reality bend and bow at each blow that was landed.

Then she saw…

Nathan, back on the street in the dark, walking with deliberate, teasing slowness to the waiting car. The car which puffed exhaust into the darkness reddened by its taillights. There would be a man inside. A big man. A violent man who held a wad of notes in his hand. Nathan would lean into the open window, talking quietly, coquettish. In for another beating and rape. How else could he make a living and feed his habit? "I like you Lady Rev," he would tell her. "But your God ain't about to send down a consignment of the good stuff, is He? I can't live wivvout the good stuff."

Eve saw light, which sculptured itself into vast figures. They were coming. They were close. The song burned her throat, the song lit her nerves. Close now. Close.

Then she saw…

Pauline, shivering in her flat, no money, no heat. Her ancient bones were fragile. She was lonely. God, so unutterably lonely. "If it wasn't for you coming to see me every week Lady Rev, I wouldn't see no one at all."

Then she saw…

The children, innocents, already corrupted by poverty and absence of hope. The little ones were the hardest to bear. The ones who were her when the Shouting People took Mum away.

The song faltered. Hands clasped about the sides of the pulpit, Eve looked down at the huge old Bible and saw…

…*Satan answered the Lord, and said, Doth Job fear God for nought? Hast not thou made an hedge about him, and about his house, and about all that he hath on every side? Thou hast blessed the work of his hands, and his substance is increased in the land. But put forth thine hand now, and touch all that he hath, and he will curse thee to thy face…*

She felt something close within her.

The song began to fade. The joy dissolved.

"Eve, please, Eve…" She was aware of Angela, shouting at her, begging her to draw open the door. She could feel the pressure wave of the angels' presence, pushing against the fabric of this reality. About to burst through –

And the Lord said unto Satan, Behold, all that he hath is in thy power; only upon himself put not forth thine hand. So Satan went forth from the presence of the Lord…

She heard the smug laughter of Satan as he presented his case. Crush her and she will curse you, God. So, she had been crushed, hadn't she? She had been broken open by the cruellest of cruelties just to win a bet, just to prove a point. She had been broken and crumpled until she would do anything for God's reward.

She had been used.

"I'm sorry," she said.

The song ceased immediately. The storm quietened and her voice sounded small and weak in the sudden silence. "I have my own war to fight. There are people who need me."

Angela took a step towards her. "Eve, please. These angels-" She waved towards the congregation, who were on their feet, their bodies bleeding away at the edges as Mum's had done a few hours before. They looked stricken, desolate.

"I'm not a pawn," Eve shouted into the shimmering body of the church. "I am a human being, not a plaything."

"Eve…"

"Let them find their own way," Eve said. "I found mine, they find theirs."

Angela's face clouded and suddenly she and the congregation were gone, replaced by a column of light from which a howl of anger raged. Eve fell back. She tried to cover her face with her arm, but it was so bright that she saw her own bones silhouetted against the glare. She grabbed at the pulpit as it dissolved beneath her. She felt her body pummelled and battered as she fell. She bounced and crashed and almost welcomed the pain. She heard the church door slam open. She heard the great crash as the window behind her exploded inwards. She covered her face as glass showered over her.

She rolled onto the hands and knees. She heard a roar and a song. She saw fire and then water flooding in through the broken window. She had to get out. She dragged herself painfully to her feet and ran towards the doorway. The door itself lay shattered in the water that swirled across the stone floor. Eve clambered over it and out into the storm.

Bent double, she ran for the road. Away from the church, which was now ablaze with light. Masonry collapsed behind her. The ground shuddered. She ran onto the lane. She didn't know if she would ever find her way out.

Then she saw Mum. Ahead. Limned by a blue glow

There's not much time, sweetheart, Mum whispered.

The road was awash now. Eve struggled in Mum's wake.

Others had her arms. She turned to see Ruth on her left, fur coat flapping open to reveal that maroon dress. She smiled and everything was all right.

Eve looked to her right and there, supporting her was a big man in a leather biker jacket. He had long hair and a wicked grin. He winked and began to sing *King of the Swingers*. Kurt, Eve realised, back from Devon. *Come on Pipkin*, he growled. *You know the words*. She sang along. Out of breath, wet and unutterably cold and tired. Ruth joined in. Mum was a long way ahead. A bluish shifting outline. Eve followed. Now shin-deep in fast-flowing water. She sang the *Jungle Book* song and kept her eyes on Mum. Always Mum.

The water was waist deep now. The going was a hard, icy wade. But Ruth and Kurt were still with her. Holding her and singing –

Eve lost her footing. She was down and there was utter darkness and the icy grip of the water. She couldn't swim. Her clothes were too heavy. She was sinking. Water filled her mouth. She wanted to breathe. She couldn't. It was dark. Black.

A hand. She couldn't see it but felt the hand grab at hers. She clutched it and knew it was Mum's hand. She held on tight and felt herself surge upwards then burst through the surface like Ariel.

Solid land.

And stillness.

It was daylight. Late according to the position of the red sun that was perched above a line of leafless trees on the far bank of a vast expanse of water. Eve knelt in the grass, looked about her and realised she was on the path beside the reservoir.

Her clothes, skin and hair were soaked. She shivered. Her teeth clattered. The water was ruffled by a gentle breeze. A dog barked. A couple, the dog's owners presumably, were hurrying towards her. The woman called out. Eve managed to raise a hand to indicate that she was unhurt then waited for them to reach her.

She looked out across the troubled water and whispered, "I love you Mum. I'll be seeing you."

Because she knew she would.

But first, whether her church took her back or not, there was work to be done.

Lightning Source UK Ltd.
Milton Keynes UK
UKHW012121030121
376189UK00001B/30